BULL'S·EYE

LITTLE·JOHN

WILL·SCARLET

KING·RICHARD

GAME

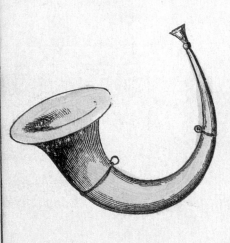

STRONGITHARM

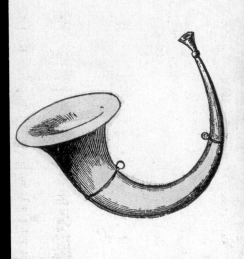

GOOD·FELLOW

ROBIN·HOOD

and his MERRY MEN

Robin
Hood

~

ROBIN HOOD

A CLASSIC ILLUSTRATED EDITION

By E. Charles Vivian

~

Compiled by Cooper Edens

chronicle books san francisco

For all the merry men – C. E.

This edition retains much of the content, spelling and grammar of the 1906 edition.

Compilation copyright © 2002 by Blue Lantern Studio.
All rights reserved.

Book design by Kristen M. Nobles.
Composition by Donna Linden.
Typeset in Mrs. Eaves and Cheltenham.
Manufactured in China.

Library of Congress Cataloging-in-Publication Data
Vivian, Evelyn Charles.
Robin Hood : a classic illustrated edition : by E. Charles Vivian ; compiled by Cooper Edens.
p. cm.
Summary: Recounts the life and adventures of Robin Hood, who, with
his band of followers, lived in Sherwood Forest as an outlaw dedicated to fighting
tyranny. Illustrations by Wyeth, Pyle, and others are compiled from other editions.
ISBN 0-8118-3399-2
1. Robin Hood (Legendary character)—Legends. [1. Robin Hood
(Legendary character)—Legends. 2. Folklore—England.]   I. Edens, Cooper. II. Title.
PZ8.1.V53 Ro 2002
398.2'0942'02—dc21
2001002713

Distributed in Canada by Raincoast Books
9050 Shaughnessy Street, Vancouver, British Columbia V6P 6E5

10 9 8 7 6 5 4 3 2 1

Chronicle Books LLC
85 Second Street, San Francisco, California 94105

www.chroniclekids.com

~ Preface ~

*obin Hood* is an excitingly vivid legend, and the timeless image of "The Prince of Thieves" has been enhanced and refined over the years by many of the world's most talented artists. Among them are N. C. Wyeth, with his splendid atmospheric brush; Howard Pyle, with his mastery of black-and-white line; Walter Crane, with his genius for decoration; Honor C. Appleton, with her whimsical pastel style; and Harry Theaker, with his flair for dramatic action.

Although successive ages have reshaped the original myths of A.D. 1200 of "The Lord of the Greenwood," the tale's heroic message of truth, justice and valor remains ageless. Robin Hood, Maid Marian, Little John, Friar Tuck, Will Scarlett, King Richard, Guy of Gisbourne and the Sheriff of Nottingham are unforgettable characters whose spirits are woven together in an intricate mosaic, part of a world where the horizon is as infinite as adventure itself.

It is my wish to further illuminate this landscape by collecting the painterly visions of these great illustrators in a single volume. At the same time, I hope to reveal the deepest secrets of Sherwood Forest, where storytellers and readers of all ages have enjoyed hiding away and rejoicing with Robin's merry band for nearly one thousand years.

—Cooper Edens

~ Table *of* Contents ~

Robin of Locksley

CHAPTER I

hite winter lay heavily on Sherwood Forest, and far across the moors to the North Country where Whitby Abbey towered over the sea. The leafless trees of the Forest bore burdens of snow, and the shrivelled tops of dead bracken stalks barely showed through the level, glaring sheet of whiteness. Winter had been cruelly long that year, and now, though the time of spring sowing was near, there was no sign of the bitter cold relaxing.

A bare stone's throw into the Forest, on the edge of the lands that Guy of Gisbourne stewarded for the rich Abbey of St. Mary's, a ragged figure skulked among the trees. Shreds of what had once been clothes hung about him as Sebald the Dolt glanced down the forest aisles, or crouched among the snow-laden undergrowth; about his legs and feet were tied wisps of dead grass for warmth, and as he moved he left little specks of red in each foot-print, for the dead stalks and twigs had pierced the soles of his numbed feet. On and on he moved, always away from the open lands and into the depths of the Forest itself.

Then he stiffened to absolute stillness, for, moving downwind, a dozen head of deer came, nosing at the snow for food, unconscious of his presence. They saw him too late for one of their number, for Sebald stepped out from behind the tree that had hidden him, lifted his bow and let fly; a young stag went down, kicking, and the rest of the deer vanished before Sebald could reach the wounded thing and end his work with a knife.

Working like a madman, he ripped the skin from the haunch of the dead beast, cut a slice of the warm flesh, and bolted it as a dog might have done. After that, he went at the carcass more carefully, cutting off the best of the meat and placing it in a pile on the snow, strip after strip of juicy venison. Then, with a cry that was more like a dog's bark, he started up, knife in hand, and faced the tall man whose shadow had fallen across him as he worked.

A young man, this newcomer, with reddish hair, a little pointed beard, and a lithe, muscular figure that betokened more than usual strength and quickness. Sebald faced him with knife upraised and terror in his gaunt face, of which every line told of hunger and fear.

"Put the knife down, Sebald," said the tall man quietly.

"Robin—Robin of Locksley!" Sebald gasped. "Master, I was starved."

"And like to be hanged," said Robin of Locksley. "For this is death, Sebald, if a forester find one head of deer taken."

"If I die of a rope, or of hunger, what difference is there?" Sebald asked doggedly. "Look you, Master Robin, when this winter began I had a wife and two little ones. But because I fell ill, a thing no serf may do, Guy of Gisbourne turned us out of our hut and gave our shelter to Walter the Bald. A serf who cannot work, said Guy, shall neither eat nor shelter on his lands, and they drove us out, the wife and the children with me, though the little ones were all unfit."

"True," said Robin, nodding. "Guy of Gisbourne is a hard man, and cruel. But it is death to touch the deer, Sebald."

"Death? What is death but a kindness?" Sebald asked. "For so my wife found it when the cold wrapped her round and she fell asleep, never to wake more in this world. So the child Freda found it, for at least she will hunger no more, and now only the boy Waltheof is left me, and he a-crying with bitter hunger, and I with naught to give him. By the Rood, Master Robin, if I hang, I hang with a full belly, and the boy shall have one more good meal!"

There was a look of pity in Robin's eyes. "Where is the boy?" he asked.

"There"—Sebald pointed along the way he had come—"in the hollow of a dead elm, wrapped in such rags as I could find him that he might not die of the cold before I could get him food."

"Then you harbour in the forest?" Robin asked.

Sebald nodded. "Else I must go back to Guy of Gisbourne, being his man," he answered. "And to go back means lashes on the back, and labour from morn to night, with more lashes at the end of it, since I am all unhandy and slow, and so they call me the dolt, Master Robin. I tell you"—his voice rose to sudden fierceness—"there is no justice for us Saxon English under these dogs of Normans!"

"It is true," Robin answered moodily. "But look you, Sebald, bring the lad with you and come to my farm. We may then decide what can best be done for you."

Sebald looked incredulous. "To your farm, Master Robin? But—but I have killed the king's deer!"

A slow smile grew in Robin's eyes. "I may have loosed a shaft or two myself, at times, good Sebald," he said, "for the deer take toll of my crops without payment. Bring the boy and come—there is at the least a shelter among the cattle where he may keep warm."

"Master Robin," said Sebald, with tears in his eyes, "well do they say you have the kindest heart 'twixt Nottingham and York."

"Tush, man!" said Robin, and turned away. "Follow when you will, and come to me. I will talk to Guy of Gisbourne, and see if I may not keep you among my men."

He turned away then, and went out from the forest and across the open to where, a couple of miles away, rose a stout wooden dwelling by the sea with its stables and byres and ricks about it. Here Robin of Locksley had lived alone since his father's death, a freeman holding his two hundred acres of land under the Abbey of St. Mary's. His grandfather, in the time of Henry the First, had been granted the tenancy of this acreage, the best of all the lands belonging to the Abbey, and when Robin's father died Guy of Gisbourne had tried vainly to thrust Robin out from his holding and take back the farm to the Abbey's use.

Now, as Robin went slowly back, thinking bitterly over the wrongs of men like Sebald, he left one track of footprints straight from the carcass of the deer to his own homestead. Presently came Sebald with his boy Waltheof, a lad of ten who shivered and even cried with the cold as he kept beside his father, and they left two more tracks in the snow.

Late that afternoon came Herbert the ranger along the edge of the forest, where Robin's lands began, and when he came to the tracks in the snow he stopped and looked down. There was the clear, long-striding track of Robin's shod feet, and Herbert passed by that, knowing whose feet had made it. Then he came on the shapeless blurs made by Sebald's grass-wrapped feet, and beside them the small indentations where the child Waltheof had walked. Herbert saw red blots in the snow, where Sebald's torn feet had bled.

"Ha!" he said. "There has been a killing here!"

So he turned into the forest, following on the tracks, and came to the hollow elm where Sebald had left his boy. Thence he followed on, and came to a place where the snow was all disturbed and thrown about, and at one place had been made into a mound on which were still the traces of Sebald's hands.

"A killing," said Herbert to himself, "and a burying, too."

He grubbed in the mound with his hands, and presently came on a two-tined antler. Grasping it, he dragged forth all that Sebald had left of the deer's carcass, and stared down at it as it lay before him.

"So!" said Herbert. "Master and man together go a-hunting! Fine news for Sir Guy—fine news! I think he will have Robin's farm at last, and for this news he will make me bailiff."

He slung the carcass across his shoulders and hurried off to Fosse Grange, as Guy of Gisbourne's strong house of stone was named, since it stood by the old fosse that runs from the Abbey of St. Mary's down toward Newark. It was all but a castle, this hold from which Guy ruled the lands of St. Mary's for Hugo de Rainault, the Norman abbot who had been granted rule of St. Mary's while Henry Curtmantle was yet alive.

A tall man and fierce was Guy, swarthy and sneering, a hater of Saxons, at whom he would jeer as he told how his grandfather had seen their sires run from Senlac when their Harold died. Even Abbot Hugo remonstrated with his steward at times, when Saxon blood ran too freely under the lashes that Guy ordered on his serfs' backs. But it was not often that Hugo said anything, for he, too, was pure Norman, and hated all Saxons in a way that no churchman should.

Into Guy's hall strode Herbert the ranger, the deer still across his shoulders. At the back of the hall was a great roaring fire of logs, before which stood Guy of Gisbourne himself, warming his hands behind his back. To him went Herbert, and laid the deer before him.

"How now, man—how now?" growled Guy. "Who has been gnawing at that meat? Why is it not a whole carcass?"

"Because Robin of Locksley has gnawed it," said Herbert.

"Ha!" said Guy, his eyes alight. "Now by the teeth of St. Peter we have him! Have you proof, Herbert?"

"Proof enough, lord," said Herbert, "for there go his footprints from where the carcass lay buried in the snow, and on across his land to his own door. There went with them the prints made by some lumbering serf and a little lad, whom he got to do the foul work with him. Proof enough, lord."

"Aye," said Guy, "proof enough. We will have Locksley back for the Abbey, and we will have, too, the hand of Master Robin chopped from him, or I think, with a word from Abbot Hugo, I may get leave to tear out his eyes. The Saxon hound has flouted us long enough, eh, Herbert?"

"Full long, Lord Guy," Herbert agreed. "And I shall be bailiff of Locksley, if it please you?"

"That is for Abbot Hugo to settle," Guy answered, "but a word from me to him shall be your reward for this news. Now away with you while I arm," Guy ordered. "Bid a dozen of our men-at-arms don their mail, and saddle me my roan horse, and I warrant you Locksley farm shall lack a tenant before the sun reddens tomorrow's snow. Hasten, good Herbert, if you would see your vacant bailiffship waiting."

He put on a suit of mail while Herbert gathered the men, and an hour before sunset they rode out from the Fosse Grange toward Locksley farm. The afternoon had gone grey and sullen, with a moist wind under which the snow began to soften to slush, and the heavily armed retainers laboured panting behind Guy's strong horse on their way to their task.

In an empty barn at Locksley farm the boy Waltheof slept amid warm straw, full-fed for the first time that winter, while Sebald dozed beside him, fed and content too. In the stout porch of the homestead stood Robin, looking up at the sky and sniffing the wind.

"A week of this," he said to himself, "and we shall be sowing our barley. It is winter's end, for a certainty."

Then he saw how, across the whiteness of the open between the farmstead and the forest edge, came a little company of men plodding through the snow. They took no note of the winding track by which they should have come, but marched straight across the ploughed fields.

"Now what do these Norman hogs want?" Robin muttered angrily. "Must they tear up my young wheat with their clumsy hooves to come at me?"

How Robin Took to the Woods

CHAPTER II

~

uy of Gisbourne and his men were still a mile away when Robin's keen eyes—such eyes as were seldom equalled for their sure vision—picked out Guy as the leader of the band, and instantly Robin linked up his glimpse of Herbert the ranger gazing at the house a while earlier, Sebald sheltering in the barn, and the carcass of the deer that Sebald had brought down. Here was danger of the worst sort springing suddenly out of the day's end, but Robin was the man to meet it.

Moving with such certainty that he seemed not to hurry at all, he stepped back into the house, buckled on his sword, and reached for his long bow and its quiver. He had Will Scarlett, his head man, armed in like fashion and out rousing the serfs while Guy and his band were still half a mile distant.

Now came Sebald, running from the barn, and he knelt before Robin as he stood in his doorway.

"Master Robin—Master Robin!" cried Sebald, "'tis I have brought this danger on you, and what is life to me? Let me give up myself to them, and appease them, if indeed they come on this matter of the slain deer."

But Robin shook his head. "Quiet, and hide, Sebald," he bade. "No man shall trust himself to me and find me fail him, be the price what it may. Back down, and I will settle with this proud steward Guy."

He had with him Will Scarlett on his right, and on his left was a fat youth with a great yew bow. This lad was Much, son of old Much the miller, who should have been helping his father at the mill, but had stolen away to drink ale with Scarlett instead, being a lazy lad by nature. Yet, having drunk Robin's ale, he took his bow and stood by Robin now trouble threatened, though he knew nothing of the nature of the trouble.

Behind these three were six of Robin's serfs who could handle either bow or quarter-staff well, since Robin always encouraged such play among them, not knowing when it might be useful. So stood the nine of them, with Sebald crouching somewhere in the rear, when Guy of Gisbourne rode into hearing, and the short winter dusk was darkening swiftly.

Robin laid an arrow on the string and held the bow lightly, as did both Scarlett and Much. Guy, who knew even then what skill the man before him had with the bow, reined in as he saw the arrows fitted.

"Robin of Locksley!" Guy cried out from the barred visor of his helm, "put down your arms and yield you all to me, steward and liege man of Abbot Hugo de Rainault, that you may suffer your due punishment!"

But Robin lifted the bow as if to take aim, and Guy's men-at-arms raised their shields as they saw it.

"Strong words, steward," Robin answered composedly. "Why and for what should we yield us?"

"For that you and your men have slain the king's deer in this forest of Sherwood," Guy called back. "And for that I declare you, Robin of Locksley, dispossessed of your holding, and to lose your right hand that you may draw bow no more."

"Without trial, steward?" Robin asked incredulously. "Without defence or question you pass judgment and sentence?"

"Trial, hind?" Guy echoed contemptuously. "What think you yourself, a baron of the realm, that you look for trial? The case is proved against you, and in the name of Abbot Hugo I do justice on you and such men as are guilty with you. Look for no trial from me!"

"Justice, you Norman thief?" Robin fired back. "I tell you, Guy of Gisbourne, since King Richard went crusading there has been no justice in our England, else evil men like you had never held place over honest people! Let your men come but another ten paces forward and some of you shall never see another day's light!"

Guy sat still on his horse for nearly a minute, then he beckoned a man of his, who came with shield raised to guard head and breast from any arrow that might fly.

"Loose me a crossbow bolt or two at that tall felon, and make us a free way into Locksley farmstead," Guy bade quietly.

The man stepped back among his fellows, and fitted a bolt to the cross-bow behind another's shield. The feathered quarrel hissed viciously, unsuspectedly, and a serf who stood between and a little behind Robin himself and Scarlett crumpled down without a sound, for the point had entered his brain. Without losing sight of Guy's movements, Robin saw the deed.

"First blood!" he cried. "Now guard you, Guy of Gisbourne, for here you shall only enter dead."

On the word, he loosed the arrow from his string, and it quivered and stuck in the visor bars of Guy of Gisbourne's helm, so strongly shot that Guy reeled and nearly fell from his saddle with the shock. And scarce had that arrow struck before a second shaft from Robin's bow went in at the neck of the cross-bowman who had shot the serf, so that the man fell with his life blood pouring out onto the snow.

"Now are we all dead men if they take us," Robin said to his followers, "so shoot hard and often till they come at us, and may the shafts pierce the mail! But do you run, Much, for this is no quarrel of yours."

"I will run," said Much, "no more than a barrel of ale untapped. For here is foul work, and I will not see it done, good master."

At that he loosed his string and sent a shaft humming, to glance off a retainer's shield harmlessly. Seven other arrows sang through the air, and one of

them found the brain of a man-at-arms, and one went through a man's calf, so that he sat down in the snow and squealed as he pulled the shaft through the wound.

"An end of three," said Robin, who grew cool now the fight had begun, "and still stands Locksley untouched." He sighted one man whose crossbow was aimed, and drove off a humming shaft that took the man in the wrist and pierced through flesh and gristle up to his elbow. "Four!" he shouted as the man turned and ran, shrieking. "How like you our welcome, steward? If you get not my right hand, you get the use of it!"

With all his force he loosed another shaft at Guy's helmet, in which the broken end of the first arrow still stuck. This second arrow struck higher, squarely in the front of the steel, which, as Robin knew, it could not pierce, but the force of it was so great that Guy of Gisbourne tumbled down into the snow and lay half stunned with the shock. And while he lay, a heap of rags shot out from behind Robin, fled across the intervening space, and a wild scream went up as Sebald the Dolt leaped on Herbert the ranger, a flying fury.

"This for my wife starved!" yelled Sebald, "and this for the child you thrust out into the cold!" And twice the knife with which he had cut up the deer flashed, while Herbert, drawing his dagger even as he was stabbed, fell dying, and thrust the dagger into Sebald's heart, so that he too fell dead, on the body of the man who had turned him out from his hut at Guy of Gisbourne's bidding.

There was a tall man of Guy's following who, when his master fell, advanced with drawn sword to stand over him, and presently Guy got on his feet and drew his sword as well. The two of them led on, both covered in mail, against the party in the shadow of the house, among whom were now seven unharmed and two dead by crossbow bolts. But Guy's party had nearly thirty yards to come, against the finest archer who ever drew bow in England, and they came heavily because of the deep, soft snow, while the great arrows hummed toward them. So it was that only these two came up, for of the rest of Guy's men three sat shielding themselves in the snow, sore wounded, and the rest lay dead.

But Guy of Gisbourne, trusting in his mail of proof, came on, as did his man, and Much, the miller's son, ran out with his quarter-staff and thwacked the man across his helm, so that he fell down senseless. But Robin stood against Guy of Gisbourne with his sword, and Scarlett and the serfs stood round to see the fight.

It was a fight of which there could besone end, for Guy of Gisbourne, heavily armed, and but lately stunned by Robin's arrow ringing against his helm, was slow, while Robin skipped round him and struck where he would. At

the last Robin lifted his sword and brought it down on the helmet so strongly that the blade snapped, and as Guy staggered Robin flung the useless hilt away and wrenched Guy's own sword out of his nerveless grasp.

"Now yield—yield to my justice, steward!" Robin bade.

"Never!" Guy grated back.

"Seize him, Scarlett," said Robin. "To it, serfs, and bind him tightly. There is a reckoning due now."

They grasped and held the man, while Robin himself went off and led in the roan war horse on which Guy had ridden. He came back with it to where they held Guy of Gisbourne prisoner. Guy was cursing most foully.

"Cease!" Robin thundered at him. "Are honest serfs to have their ears befouled by such a man as this! By the Rood, steward, death is but an inch distant from thee."

"Kill and make an end," said Guy. "I had as well be dead as shamed."

"Not so," said Robin, "for there has been enough of killing this day, and the shaming is not yet finished. Hark, steward! For this killing I am an outlawed man, and these poor loyal souls with me—that much I know. Abbot Hugo will welcome the excuse, but I have it in mind to send him a messenger of this day's work before the price is set on my head. Lift him on the horse, Scarlett, and face his head toward its tail."

This they did, Scarlett and the serfs heaving most mightily until they had the kicking, struggling steward placed. Then they brought ropes at Robin's bidding, and Much, the miller's son, lashed Guy's feet tightly under the horse, so that he could not move to dismount.

"Now, steward," said Robin, "ride you thus to Abbot Hugo, or first to your own grange, I care not which. But say to Abbot Hugo that from this day he may take Locksley farm, to the use of the fat thieves that wear the cowl in St. Mary's under him. Tell him, too, that he and his shall pay for the farm, for from this day I declare war on him and all his kind, as on you and your kind, who from behind stone walls ravage and imperil honest men."

"Honest!" Guy roared savagely.

"Aye," said Robin, "a word to anger you, since honesty and you are such strangers. I tell you and your abbot, steward, that for this day's work I will have a reckoning against you oppressors who thrust women and children out to starve in the cold, and die. Scarlett, give him a rein in each hand and let him go."

Then Robin picked up the steward's sword and struck the horse across his flank with the flat of it, and Guy rode off, facing toward them, into the darkness, shouting threats of the vengeance of Abbot Hugo until he was out of hearing.

"Now," said Robin, "there is much to do. Let us bury these our men who died for us, but leave Guy's men till he come again."

This they did, and when it was over Robin gathered his men in the great front room of the farmstead, and spoke to them by the flickering rushlight while they sat over meat and ale.

"With the dawn comes Guy again," he told them, "and for to-day's work there is torture and a hanging for every man of us, if they find us."

"We will stand by you, master," Scarlett said.

"Aye, but not on a scaffold," Robin answered. "As for me, I am for the depths of Sherwood, where no man may track or find us. A free life and an open, lads, with wood a-plenty for fires to warm us, and to roast our meat as we bring it down. War on those who have drained our lives of all but labour that they may fatten in ease—who comes with me?"

"I," said Scarlett and Much together, and then all the rest answered too. They were but nine, all told, that followed Robin of Locksley to the forest at first, but they were brave men all, as he knew.

"I thank you, friends," he said, "and look for a better life there than we have known yet. Now to take all that we can carry for our comfort, and away. This thaw will hide our tracks. But first do you, Much, take the lad Waltheof to your father's mill, and there leave him to be tended."

By midnight Locksley homestead stood empty.

How Robin Dined with the Sheriff

CHAPTER III

~

t was mid-March when Robin of Locksley, not yet known as Robin Hood, took to the depths of Sherwood, knowing that a price would be set on his head for the killing of Guy of Gisbourne's men, and still more for the way in which he had shamed Guy himself. Robin, who knew the forest wilds better than any man of his time, led his nine men to a glade in a valley where a cave at the side gave them shelter, a clear stream provided water, and the deer, plentiful enough, served for meat. For the rest, they had brought all the stores there were in Locksley, and for the time were fed and content.

Yet Robin knew well that the deer alone could not keep them, and he remembered, too, his promise to Guy of Gisbourne that Abbot Hugo should pay for the farm he coveted. So he gathered his nine followers, since no more had yet come to join them, and declared his purpose to them.

"We are free men, all," he told them, "and if I will you to obey me, it is for your own good. There are no more serfs among us, nor shall be. Now look you, my merry men, that you do no harm to yeomen, or to them that till with the plough, or to the knight or squire who is kind to the poor. But these bishops and abbots who rob the poor, and the high sheriffs who bind and beat them, cropping their ears and cruelly ill-treating them, these you shall lighten of their ill-gotten gains. Yet, by the Virgin, you shall never do harm to any woman in the land."

This was the law of the band that Robin formed, and, but a day after he had made it, he and his men lay along the road to Nottingham, being out on a hunt, when the Prior of Newark came down the road with half a dozen baggage mules and monks to lead them, and only a couple of armed retainers of the Priory for guard. Since these two took to their horses' heels at sight of nine resolute bowmen and their hooded leader—for Robin had drawn a hood over his face before he showed himself—there was no fighting. But there were two kegs of good wine, and four hundred marks in gold that the Prior had taken as rent for his lands, and a store of brown cloth, and bags of good white flour, which Robin counted up while the Prior and his monks stood by, bound with the ropes by which they had led the mules.

"A discerning man, this Prior," said Robin. "If we had told him our needs he could not have served us better."

"You hooded rascal!" the Prior stormed, "you dare not rob the Church."

"No, Prior," said Robin, "but a fat thief who disgraces the Church, as I will rob all like you. Now we will bind you all on your mules, and give you a hand apiece free to guide them home, where you may tell that Robin i' the Hood begins his rule in Sherwood Forest, and war on all oppressors of the poor."

And, while the disgruntled Prior and his monks made their sorry way on toward Newark, Robin and his men retreated to their fastness with this welcome spoil. From that day the great outlaw began to be known as Robin i' the Hood, or Robin Hood.

Now, lying up in the forest, they had no news of what went on in the outer world, and Robin himself determined to get news in some way. The spring was still young when, on the track between Mansfield village and Nottingham town, he met with the potter of Mansfield, who rode in his cart with a load of pots for sale in Nottingham.

"A good day to you, potter," said Robin. "'Tis a good load you carry."

"Good enough," retorted the potter, driving on. But Robin got in the middle of the track, and the horse stopped.

"Out, fellow," said the potter, "lest I drive over you."

"Not so, potter," said Robin, "but let us drive a bargain. I have need of that horse and cart, and the pots as well. I will turn potter for the day, and see how goes the world in Nottingham."

"Now I am a ruined man," said the potter, for he saw Scarlett and some others of Robin's men lurking beside the way, and knew himself among outlaws. "For if I lose my horse and cart—"

"You shall lose nothing by me," Robin promised. "Sell me the pots at the price you would ask in Nottingham, and I will leave with you two gold marks as surety for the horse and cart. But lend me too your clothes with the potter's clay on them, lest I should be known in Nottingham as Robin i' the Hood himself."

"Robin i' the Hood?" the potter echoed, amazed. "He who with a band of fifty knaves robbed the Prior of Newark?"

"Fifty," said Robin, "no, but it will be a hundred when the Prior has told the tale a few times more. But lend me the clothes and the horse and cart, potter, for there is no help for it."

Contented by the sight of the two gold marks and the price of his pots, the potter made the exchange, and Robin drove off to Nottingham, leaving the potter with his men till he should return. Having reached the town marketplace, he set up his wares at less than half their usual price, and, since one woman told another of the rare bargains to be had, he soon sold all the cheaper stuff. But he had left a dozen or so of large dishes and plates, the best of the stock.

Now across the market stood the great house of Robert de Rainault, Sheriff of Nottingham and brother to Hugo de Rainault, Abbot of St. Mary's. Robin put his wares in a basket, went across the market-square, and knocked at the sheriff's door. Presently came a serving woman.

"Having traded well in your market," said Robin, with a bow, "I bring these poor vessels as a present for Mistress de Rainault, if she will accept them as a gift."

"A gift from you?" the woman asked.

Robin nodded. "From the potter of Mansfield," he answered, and, leaving the basket, went back to his cart and waited.

Presently the woman came across the square and found him by his cart.

"Good potter," she said, "my master thinks it a right welcome gift, for we were short of dishes, and he asks that you come and take meat at his board."

"Gladly," said Robin, "especially if there be ale as well as meat, for crying pots for sale is dry work."

He followed the woman into de Rainault's house, well knowing that its owner would hang him yards high if he guessed his identity. There they gave him a seat at the great board, below the salt, with de Rainault's men, and piled his plate high, with a great horn of ale beside it. Meanwhile de Rainault, seated above the salt with his wife and some friends, talked, which was what Robin wanted.

"Forty gold marks," said the Sheriff, "and the crier shall cry it in the town to-day."

"Forty?" said one of his friends. "A high price for any man's head."

"But this is a dangerous man," the Sheriff explained. "He killed seven of Guy of Gisbourne's armed followers with his own hand, and made Guy a laughingstock to boot. And with a great band of seventy or more followers he robbed the Prior of Newark of all the good man possessed."

"Good," said Robin to himself, "the fifty have grown to seventy, now."

"A dangerous villain," said the Sheriff's wife, "let us hope he do not come to Nottingham."

"Let him come!" cried de Rainault. "I would capture him myself, and give you half the forty marks reward for new dresses."

"Would you though?" said Robin to himself, smiling.

"And to-day," the Sheriff went on, "he shall be cried through the streets of Nottingham as wolf's head, outlaw, for any man to take or kill at sight, with forty marks reward for proof of his death or for his body if captured alive. We must rid our good county of such pests."

Robin got up from the board, having eaten enough, and marched up to stand before the Sheriff, to whom he bowed low.

"Thanks for the good food, Lord Sheriff," he said, "and I will now get back to my trade."

"Who are you, varlet, and what is your trade?" the Sheriff asked haughtily.

"And I trust your noble dame will find my poor pots welcome," Robin concluded, without answering the question.

"Ha!" said de Rainault, "'tis our potter! The dishes were right welcome, potter, and I trust you have fed well at my board. But now, where do you go?"

"Back to Mansfield, to make more pots, for I have sold all my stock," Robin answered.

"Look to your going, then," the Sheriff warned him, "for there is a most pestilent rogue loose in Sherwood who will rob you of every groat if he find you. We have put out a reward of forty gold marks for his head, and Guy of Gisbourne is assembling a band to scour the forest for him next week and root him out. If you get news of him, 'twould be worth a silver mark here."

"Lord Sheriff," said Robin meekly, "if I can earn that silver mark, I will come back with the news. But I am a man of peace, and trust I do not fall in with this outlaw. I give you good day."

"A good day to you, master potter, and our thanks for the dishes," said the Sheriff's wife. Robin bowed to her and went on his way.

Little John's Quarter-Staff

CHAPTER IV

~

obin Hood drove out from Nottingham, knowing that he must take his men deep into Sherwood, since Guy of Gisbourne was coming to capture them, and knowing, too, that any man who could might kill him, and get forty gold marks, a fortune in those days, for the killing. But he whistled blithely enough as he drove along; in Sherwood was safety, as he knew, and he had anticipated being outlawed when he left Locksley Farm for Abbot Hugo to take back.

When he had got back his own clothes from the potter, and handed over the horse and cart, he bade Will Scarlett lead his men back to their hiding place in the forest, and, taking his bow and the sword he had captured from Guy of Gisbourne, set out alone for a look at his lands of Locksley. He reached them in mid-afternoon, to see that Guy's men were already sowing the barley he had hoped to sow, for spring was advancing fast now, and the trees had begun to put on their spring coats.

Again, as he watched and thought of the price set on his head, he renewed in his heart the promise he had made to Guy that the Abbot should pay in full for the farm, as should all fat abbots and great men who thrived on the poverty of others. Henceforth the greenwood must be his home, he knew, and he could never go back to Locksley.

He turned back and made his way along a little track that would lead him to his band. This track took him down a wooded slope to a stream, across which a felled tree made a footbridge. As he neared the bridge from his side of the stream, a great, tall man came down to it from the other side. The tall man carried nothing but a big quarter-staff of oak, and he hurried, as did Robin, to be first to get to the bridge. Each of them set foot on it at the same time, and neither would draw back.

"Out!" said the giant. "Out, little man, and make way for me, unless you want a ducking in the stream."

"Not so fast," said Robin, "or I will do the ducking myself, and leave you with a wet coat."

The great man swung his heavy quarter-staff within a foot of Robin's nose. "Get back!" he shouted, "before I hurt you."

But Robin, at the swing of the great staff, laid an arrow on his bow-string, at which the big man raised his staff threateningly.

"Dare but attempt to draw that string and this staff shall crack your skull!" he threatened.

"Why, fool," said Robin contemptuously, "this arrow would be through your heart before the staff could reach me."

The giant dropped his staff and leaned on it as he stood on the bridge. "Now this is a coward facing me, for I have no bow," he said. "If I had, I could teach you how to shoot an arrow."

"No coward I," Robin retorted. "Had I such a staff as that, I would teach you more about quarter-play than you could ever teach me of archery."

"Go and cut a staff, then," said the giant, "for there are plenty about. I will wait here, and we will fight on the bridge. The one who thwacks the other into the stream shall have right to cross first."

"Now this is a good fighting man," said Robin, "and one I like. Wait here, and mind my bow for me, big fellow."

He put down his bow and quiver on the bridge while the giant sat down with a grin on his face, having found a fighter like himself. Then with his hunting-knife Robin cut himself a great staff, trimmed it to his liking, and returned, at which the giant stood up and the fight began.

From the attitude of his opponent the giant could see that he had no easy task, and he began cautiously, feeling his way to find what Robin knew of quarter-staff play. He soon found out, for in less than a minute Robin gave him a thwack across the shoulders that shook him into rage, and after that they guarded and parried each other's blows till the great staves hummed, and the giant, skillfully evading the blows aimed at him, fairly danced on the bridge, until he nearly danced himself into the water.

"Keep at it, bantam," he roared, "the lesson is only just begun. Good guard, but I am only just warming to it. Look to your head!"

A whizzing blow just shaved Robin's ear, and he retaliated with a thwack that the giant caught on his staff, so that the two staves rattled together as Robin gave back a pace. Then he leaped in the air as the giant tried to sweep his feet from under him, and by this time the two of them were panting for breath, for the play was fast and furious.

"Truce!" Robin called, and stepped back. The giant leaned on his staff, puffing for breath.

"I was about to call it myself," he gasped. "By my soul, a right good fight, this, but I will never give way to let you cross the bridge."

"Have at it, then," said Robin, and they set to again.

Parry and thrust and blow gave neither the advantage for a time, but then Robin caught the giant another mighty buffet which came down on his head and would have broken the skull of a weaker man.

"Take that," said Robin, "and let me across this bridge."

"Never," roared the big man, and, twirling his great staff, he came on again. Playing skillfully, in spite of the buzzing in his head after Robin's blow, he parried another like it and gave Robin a mighty thwack which made him lose his foothold and tumbled him into the stream with a great splash.

Robin Hood · meeteth · the · tall
Stranger · on · the · Bridge

"Now," said the big man gleefully, "I cross the bridge first. But where are you gone?"

"Here, swimming with the stream," Robin answered from the water, as he caught at the log bridge and drew himself up. The giant leaned down and gave him a hand, roaring with laughter at his dripping figure. Then they sat down on the bridge together.

"Giant," said Robin, "never met I such a fighter with the staff. I yield you best at it."

"'Twas a joyous fight," said the giant, "and I would I might meet such a fighter every day, but good men are scarce. We will have a match with the bow some day when I find you dry—but at a target, not at each other."

"Willingly," Robin answered. "But how do they call you, big man?"

"As a rule," said the giant, "they call me too late for a good meal, and so I am often hungry, but my name is John of Mansfield, since I come from that village."

"And what do you here in the forest?" Robin pursued.

"Hide," said John. "I was Ralph of Mansfield's man, and one morning I slept too late. Ralph is a cruel master, and he ordered me forty lashes for my sleep, but I took the whip and stunned the man that should have laid them on, and then there was naught for it but to flee."

"So!" said Robin. "Here is another like Guy of Gisbourne."

John laughed. "As like as a pea to another pea," he agreed. "They say that a man named Robin took Guy and tied him facing his horse's tail, and took to the forest after, being outlawed."

"They say that, do they?" Robin asked, smiling.

"Aye, and this same Robin took a band and spoiled the fat Prior of Newark not long after. A right good man he must be, one after my own heart, and I would join with him if I could."

"For what purpose?" Robin asked.

"I would put my hand in his and be his man," said John. "For look you, archer, I will give no man best with the quarter-staff, but a man may not earn his living by play with the staff alone, and this forest is an uneasy place if one has no companions."

"Put your hand in mine then," Robin said, and held out his hand.

The giant stared at him.

"Come," said Robin, "there is yet a keg of the Prior of Newark's wine left in our lodgings, and good white bread to go with the venison. And I think Will Scarlett shot a boar yesterday—succulent pork, John, with the crackling done to a turn."

"You—you are this Robin?" John asked, amazed.

Robin laughed. "And a-wanting good men," he answered. "Say, you tiny little man, how shall it be? Will you put your hand in mine and join with me now the chance is here?"

"Willingly, and now," said John. "The crackling on the pork decides me, if nothing else would. And that keg, Robin, let us away to where you keep these good things and drink each other's health, for you being all wet outside must be dry within, after our great fight. And mayhap, when we have finished the pork, there will be a half haunch of venison or thereabouts as a snack for me."

"A half haunch?" Robin echoed. "Man, would you keep my men hunting both night and day to feed you full?"

"Good Robin, if I come to be your man, I will earn my keep," said John. "Trust me for that."

Robin nodded gravely. "There will be time for that, for Guy of Gisbourne comes with a band of men to scour the forest for me before a week is out," he said. "It will be no life of ease, I warn you."

"Give me a good bow and feed me well," said John, "and I will draw a string with your best against Guy and his men. But let us away, Robin, for the crackling on the pork draws me most mightily."

"Then let us go, little John of Mansfield," Robin agreed, "for we have a full mile to trudge to where that crackling lies. And you being but a man and a half in size, and maybe three men in appetite, we will name you Little John."

So they went on, and Robin's men gave their new comrade a good welcome when Robin had told them of the fight on the bridge and laughed at his own discomfiture at the game of quarter-staff. And this was one of the qualities that made him dear to his followers, that he could take a beating in good part, and recognize all the skill of the man who beat him, bearing no malice.

There were then in Sherwood scores of masterless men like John of Mansfield, and when they heard how Robin had spoiled the Prior of Newark they sought him out with a view to joining him. But he would take only the best and most skillful at arms, and these he made swear to follow the rules he had given to his nine men from Locksley. Even so, he had many more than nine men when Guy of Gisbourne came hunting him in Sherwood.

His band was not yet at the full strength to which it grew later, nor was his fame yet great, but men heard of what he had done to Guy of Gisbourne and the Prior, and there were few who thought it worthwhile to try for the forty marks set as price on his head.

Guy of Gisbourne's First Attempt

CHAPTER V

~

alf-way between Ollerton and Worksop is a spot on which once stood the rich Abbey of St. Mary's, where Hugo de Rainault ruled in Robin Hood's time. A little to the north of it, on an eminence that commanded all the country round, rose the great castle of Belame, from which Isambart de Belame, as bad a baron as ever followed such a bad prince as John, terrorized the lands about him. But there was a sort of bargain between Isambart and Abbot Hugo by which they divided the country between them; Hugo's church lands lay south and east, while Isambart took tribute up toward the Yorkshire border, and, in return for the benefit of the Church, helped Hugo in any need.

It was in the time of Isambart's father, as bad a man as himself, that the castle of Belame first got its nickname of Evil Hold, and so it was known all over the countryside when Robin took to Sherwood's depths. Men travelled very little in those days, but many who had never seen Evil Hold knew its reputation, and knew that to fall into Isambart's clutches was to give up all hope, and generally to say good-bye to life as well.

Yet Isambart was useful to Abbott Hugo, so there was peace between them, no matter how heinous Isambart's crimes were against the people who fell into his grasp. And when Guy of Gisbourne had been shamed and the Prior of Newark had suffered loss at Robin's hands, Abbot Hugo sent for Isambart to meet him and Guy, to make an end of the bold outlaw.

The three held a council in the Abbot's pleasant room in St. Mary's Abbey. Hugo was a great, fat man who always spoke Norman-French, though he understood English. Isambart was tall and lean and fierce, with a nose like a hawk's beak, and cruel eyes, and he grinned at the tale of how Guy had been tied on his horse by Robin at Locksley farm.

But he ceased to grin when Hugo told how the Prior of Newark had been robbed by a band of nearly a hundred outlaws under Robin Hood. For the number of men Robin had had with him grew greater every time the Prior told the tale.

"It is ever the same," said the Abbot. "Let a man but get up and do some evil deed against us and the outlaws of the Forest will swarm round him. Now, as you know, Sir Isambart, we have few men-at-arms belonging to our Abbey."

"Some five or six less than you had before they tried to take this Robin of Locksley," Isambart agreed.

"And Guy, here, knows his way in Sherwood Forest," the Abbot pursued. "Now it is my wish that you lend me, say, thirty well-armed men to add to my own, and with Guy at their head they will root out this Robin before he becomes dangerous to us."

"And what do I get if I lend you thirty men?" Isambart asked.

"You get the honour of helping Holy Church at need," said the Abbot.

Isambart smiled craftily. "A cheap reward," he remarked. "Good Hugo, since my wife died I am a lonely man in my castle of Belame. If I give you my help in this matter, you shall give me your ward Marian, who is under shelter at Kirklees with the Abbess there, but is none the less yours to give to any man you will."

"Ha!" said the Abbot. "This is a great reward you ask."

"Truly great," Isambart agreed, "for you thought to make a nun of Marian and take all her broad lands to add to yours of St. Mary's. But she is too beautiful to be a nun, and would better be wife to me."

"It is too much to ask," the Abbot said.

"So be it," Isambart replied, "but when this bold outlaw is burning your Abbey over your head you will wish you had paid the price of my thirty men before he set fire to you."

"Enough," said the Abbot hastily. "You shall have the maid when Guy here has done his work. It is a bargain."

"That is not the bargain," Isambart insisted. "If I lend you thirty of my men to follow Guy, then I shall have the maid whether he make an end of this Robin or no. Let that be the bargain."

The Abbot reflected that with the score of men he had himself, and Isambart's thirty, he would have a band that could easily put an end to a few ragged outlaws. It was safe enough.

"So be it, Sir Isambart," he said. "Give me the men to follow my steward on this hunt, and then Guy shall escort the maid Marian to your castle, to be married to you in the chapel there with him for witness."

"You shall have the men in three days," Isambart promised.

They held this council on the day that Robin sold pots in Nottingham, and Isambart kept his promise, so that thirty stout fellows, well armed, reported themselves to Guy of Gisbourne outside his stone grange three days later. Then Guy gathered his men, and they set out for the depths of Sherwood.

They took two days' provisions with them, knowing that the hunt might be a long one. For Sherwood in those days was ten times the size it is now, a place of thickets and gloomy depths, and caves in which men might hide, and deep hollows where, according to legend, sprites and elves lurked, with strange spirit shapes that could mislead travellers, and even turn them into animal forms if they chose. It was an age of superstition in which men believed in anything, from fairies to dragons.

Robin, who had explored the depths of the Forest from his boyhood, spied on the gathering at Guy's grange from a distance, and knew how many men Guy had with him, and he determined to lead them such a dance as had never been known in the Forest. He had now over thirty followers, all men that he had proved, and had no fear of Guy's band, who, heavily armed as they were, would soon tire on the tracks he meant them to follow.

When, a little after sunrise, Guy led his party from the grange, Robin himself and Little John lay up to watch them march. The two saw where the party would enter the forest, and Robin hurried to get on the track, where he laid a naked sword, with its point toward the way Guy and his men must come. Then he and Little John hid themselves.

Presently came Guy, fully armed and with his visor down, riding at the head of his men. He saw the sword lying on the grass, and bade one of his men pick it up. But, as the man stooped, a voice screeched out of the forest depths.

"Put down that sword! Dead men have no use for swords."

The man started back as if the sword had been a snake, frightened by the unearthly screech, which he took for the voice of one of the spirits of the forest.

"Pick it up, man!" Guy roared. "Art afraid of a voice?"

The man bent again to pick up the sword, and again the voice called out as he stooped.

"It is death to touch it—death to touch it!"

Again the man left the sword alone. "Master," he said, trembling, "I dare not. It is a fairy sword."

"You are a fairy fool!" Guy snorted. "Hold my horse for me."

In his full armour he started to dismount, to pick up the sword himself. Just as he lifted his leg over the high cantle of his saddle, a great arrow hummed out of the forest and rattled on the side of his helmet, so that he lost his balance and crashed to the ground like a crate of ironware. And then with yells his men took to their heels and bolted back, for the sword began to move of itself across the grass.

Guy, unharmed, got to his feet and, staring stupidly at the moving sword, saw that it was tied to a fine cord which led into the forest depths beside the track. He rushed at it, grasped, and snapped the cord.

"A trick—a trick!" he shouted. "Back here to me, you fools, and follow that cord! We will have the knave at the end of it!"

He ran into the thicket, not knowing that Robin had run the cord round a tree and back across the track to its other side, a little higher up. A dozen of Guy's men, recovering from their fear, followed their master; but they had nothing to guide them now, for Robin had pulled the cord out of their sight and wound it in.

As they beat the bushes with their swords and thrust behind trees, there came suddenly a screech of laughter from behind, an elfish noise that set them shuddering.

"Ha, ha, ha! Ha, ha, ha, ha, ha!" The voice echoed among the trees, so that they could not tell whence it came, nor who made it. Even Guy of Gisbourne crossed himself in fear.

"It is the pixies of the wood," said one scared man to another. "Now we shall be led in circles till we drop and die of starvation, for once the pixies get at a man in Sherwood there is no escape for him."

"Silence, fool!" roared Guy. "It is but this pestilent outlaw tricking us. Let me but get on my horse and come at him and I will put an end to his tricks. Back to the path, and keep together."

He assembled the band again, all but two who, once they had started running, never stopped till they got back to St. Mary's grange, where they gave out that Guy of Gisbourne and all his men were bewitched and lost in Sherwood's depths, past any man's finding. But Guy led on along the track, and his men took heart and followed.

Now they came to a place where the track became very narrow between great trees, so that at one point they had all to go in single file. Guy himself went first on his horse, and his men followed on foot, one by one. The place was very gloomy because of the interlacing branches of the great trees over them. Here, as the last man waited his turn to move, a rope suddenly coiled down from the branches, with a loop at its end which tightened round his neck and drew him up, but not before he let out a wild yell of fear.

The men just in front, seeing him suddenly dangling in mid-air in the gloom, bolted forward, and it was a couple of minutes or more before any could come to his rescue. Then one of them ran and cut him down with a sword, and he tumbled on the grass, half strangled, and unable to speak for the time.

"Up that tree, one of you," Guy shouted, "and get me the villain who dropped the rope. Swift, before he escapes!"

But all they found was the other end of the rope knotted round a branch, and no sign of any man. So far, except for this half-strangled man, they had come to no real harm, but every man of them devoutly wished himself out of this haunted forest.

And, in a glade a quarter of a mile away, Robin and his men were splitting their sides with laughter at the dance they were leading Guy and his party, for this was sport after their own hearts.

"Now for the bridge," Robin said. "If they go on, they must come to the bridge. It is ready for them, eh, Will?"

"Ready and waiting, Robin," said Will Scarlett, with a chuckle.

They went on through the forest to a point where two logs formed the main supports of a rough bridge across a stream, with smaller logs laid cross-wise on them to make the roadway, and trampled brushwood on the cross pieces for footing. Here, again, Robin had had his men loop ropes round one end of each great log, and now they took their stand at the other ends of the two ropes, ten to each, well hidden in thickets. There they waited till Robin himself, on the watch for Guy's party, should give the word.

Marching solidly together, and searching every thicket on each side of the track, Guy and his men came down to the stream. The rough bridge was strong enough to take them all at once, and Guy rode down on to it, peering into the woods on the other side. He was half-way across, with a dozen of his men around him, when a voice called "Heave!"

Then Robin's two parties pulled on their ropes with all their force, and the two supporting logs of the bridge, with the earth dug away from their ends in readiness, parted, one upstream and one down, so that the bridge itself collapsed, and with a mighty splash Guy on his horse and his dozen followers went into the depths of the stream. If it had not been for his horse, which pulled him ashore on the bank from which he had come, Guy of Gisbourne would have been drowned in his heavy armour, and of his twelve followers one was drowned in the swift current before his fellows could rescue him. They had all they could do to scramble out themselves.

Now, while Guy stood shivering and cursing on the bank, with no bridge by which to cross, three men stepped into view on the far side of the stream. In the middle was Robin Hood himself, with Little John on his right and Will Scarlett on his left.

"At them with your crossbows, you fools!" yelled Guy, soaked and wrathful. "There stands the outlaw himself—will you let him jeer at you in safety?"

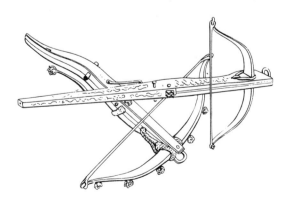

"Hold!" Robin cried. "My men are all about you, and the first man who aims a bolt dies. So far, Guy of Gisbourne, I and my men have but played with you. Go back to safety before we turn our play to earnest, if you would get out from Sherwood alive."

"Go back? Never!" shouted Guy. "Never till we have hanged you, rascal, and made an end of your tricks in Sherwood."

"Then look to yourselves," Robin answered. "We give you till night-fall to withdraw from the forest. If you are still within it then, it shall be at your peril."

"Shoot them down, men!" Guy shouted. "Here—give me a crossbow."

But before a bolt could be laid to string, the three had vanished, and there was the broad stream between their hiding-places and Guy of Gisbourne's men. All the forest was silent and empty again, without a sign of enemy, though Guy and his men felt that they were watched by invisible eyes.

How Guy's Band Went Home

CHAPTER VI

~

ow Guy got all his band together again, and cursed them soundly, though he might just as well have cursed himself. He was shivering wet inside his armour, and very angry at the way in which Robin had fooled him. When he counted up his band he found he was three men short.

"This," he told the rest, "comes of being afraid of a pack of fools who would run at the sight of our swords. I would have you know, louts, that all that has scared you has been this Robin Hood and his tricks, but now we will take no more note of his knavish follies. Spread out along the banks of this stream and find a ford, for we cross it and hunt him down ere we go back from Sherwood."

They searched up and down the stream, and saw no man on either bank, for Robin had said that he would give them till nightfall to withdraw, and he kept his word even with his enemies. A party of Guy's men found a place shallow enough for them to cross the stream, and they waded through, all tired now, and hungry as well. But Robin and his merry men sat in a glade a mile away, and ate and drank in comfort, all but the couple who watched to report on Guy of Gisbourne's movements.

All that afternoon Guy's men searched the greenwood in vain, for Robin's men fell back before them into the forest depths. They were miles from their starting point when night came, and Guy, halting them in an open glade, bade them eat of the provisions they had brought, after which he set a guard of fifteen men for the night.

"For we go not out from this forest till we have made an end of Robin Hood and his band," he told his men. "Already they have come to an end of their devices and flee before us in fear."

"Ha, ha, ha, ha!" came a mocking laugh from a nearby thicket.

They loosed a dozen crossbow bolts into the thicket, and searched it thoroughly afterward, but could find no sign of any man.

"Nothing but a blue jay squawking," Guy said scornfully. "You are as scared as a nest of mice, though the only man among you that took any harm is he who drowned himself. Now build a great fire in this glade and set the guard, for it grows dark."

This was done, and while the fifteen men patrolled the edges of the glade, the others tried to rest, uneasily enough. Just when it was fully dark, and they were beginning to doze off, came a series of unearthly moans out of the forest, and they started up in affright.

"The pixies are abroad," one whispered to another. "Now are we all lost men."

"They say the dragon of Dark Mere haunts nearby this place," said another, "and gobbles men as a swallow gulps down flies. Hark!"

For a weird scream followed on the moaning, and they all sat up and grasped at their arms. Elfin laughter, echoing from all points at once, came after the screaming.

"I will give two tall candles to St. Hubert's shrine if ever I get safe out of this," said one great fellow, crossing himself devoutly.

"Silence, loon!" Guy commanded, though his own voice shook with fright at the forest hauntings. "It is but these outlaws at their tricks again."

And, though he only half believed what he said, he lay down to try and get some sleep, being now somewhat dried after his ducking, though he was shivery in the night air in his cold armour, and dared not remove a piece more than his helmet. But there came no more noises, and presently they all rested until it was time for fifteen more of them to be roused to relieve the first watch.

It was just on midnight when one of these men of the second watch came to Guy of Gisbourne and saw that he was awake.

"Master," said the man, "see there—through the forest!"

Guy sat up and looked, seeing through the foliage a flickering glow, as of a distant fire. He scratched his head and got to his feet.

"Now we have them," he said, "for that will be the fire round which Robin and his men sleep this night, thinking us afraid to move. Rouse all the band, bid them make no sound, and we will away after this great thief and make an end of him."

But on second thought he left behind the more heavily armed and clumsy men of his band, lest they should make a clatter in the woods and rouse the outlaws' camp too soon. Six and thirty men in all went creeping through the forest in the end, bent on surprising Robin and his men asleep.

They stole on among the trees, feeling their way in the darkness, and saw at last how a great fire burned in the midst of a wide glade, with, on the far side of the fire, the figures of a score or more men showing indistinctly in the flickering light as they lay asleep, and one who paced back and forward like a sentry—it was Much, the miller's son, whom Robin had set to this task. The light was too uncertain to try a shot at him, and Guy mustered his men at the edge of the glade, reckoning that if he caught all the band asleep but one, it would be an easy matter to overcome them before they could get to their arms.

The fire was a score of yards away, and the sleeping figures perhaps some ten yards more. When Guy had all his men together, and had bidden them each mark his man, he leaped out into the open waving his sword, as signal for them to charge down on the outlaws' camp, but he cried no word to give warning to the sleepers.

After him came his men, charging out, eager to end this business in the forest depths and get back to the open lands they knew. But half-way to the fire first one and then another went thundering to the ground, for Robin had had his men stretch ropes, a little less than knee-high, across the glade, and in the darkness the ropes were invisible as they hung, tied from one great tree to another. Guy's men fell on each other, and cursed and swore and even fought each other, thinking Robin's men were on them, while the sleeping forms beyond the fire never stirred, since they were but stuffed dummies that Robin had had laid there to bait the trap.

But, while Guy's men were all tangled up with the slack ropes, and a good two-thirds of them were rolling on the turf helplessly, out from either side leaped Robin and his men, armed with great cudgels. Robin himself knocked Guy of Gisbourne insensible with a mighty blow, and so well did they all use their cudgels that, by the time Guy came to again, he and his men were all trussed as tightly as cooking fowls.

"Now, Scarlett," said Robin, "do you and Much mind these cockerels, and stun any one of them who makes a noise. The rest of you, to their camp with me."

Vanishing in the forest, they rushed Guy's guards with their cudgels, and, being three to one now, made them all prisoners without the loss of a man, though Little John got a black eye from one fellow whom he tackled. Then they took these eleven others back to where Guy and the main body lay bound.

"Pile all their arms by the dummies there," Robin ordered, "and strip off their armour and pile it there too, with special care for Guy of Gisbourne's iron suit, which might fit me at need."

So this was done, while Guy of Gisbourne cursed most foully till Robin threatened to hang him unless he held his tongue.

"Now," said Robin, " 'tis a warm night, and good clothes are scarce in Sherwood. Strip every man of them of all but his shirt, and do you, Little John, Scarlett and Much, join me with your bows, to shoot down anyone who resists."

But Guy's men, unarmed and defenceless, had no heart for resistance, and presently seven and forty sorry figures stood, each with nothing on but a shirt, his hands tied behind him. Robin, taking his sword, strode up to Guy of Gisbourne.

"Steward," he said fiercely, "had you been in our place, you had hanged us every one, as I know well. I have taken you and your fifty men to show you and your proud Abbot who is lord in Sherwood, and I tell you that if he send you against me again, I will come out and burn your grange about your ears. I have taken no life of your men's lives, and, save that you will have sore feet before you win home, I have harmed no man of you. Get you with these men back to those who sent you, and tell them the welcome Robin Hood made for you and your men in Sherwood."

So it happened that seven and forty sorry men, each with nothing on but a shirt, went out weary and hungered and with bleeding feet from Sherwood Forest about the hour of dawn, and each man had his hands tied behind his back.

Some went with Guy of Gisbourne to his grange, and some went straight to St. Mary's Abbey for food and clothing, and some there were who went to Isambart de Belame at Evil Hold, to tell him what sort of man was this Robin Hood who ruled in Sherwood.

They say that Abbot Hugo raved in wrath, and Isambart de Belame cursed his men till he was black in the face, while Guy of Gisbourne hid in his grange till his sore feet had healed, and told no man what he thought of that night's work. But from Newark in the south to Sheffield, and even to far-away York itself, men roared with laughter at the tale of seven and forty men tramping out from Sherwood in their shirts, beaten and bound by stout Robin Hood and his band.

And, after this, Robin had more offers of service in his band than he wanted, so that he was able to pick and choose only the very best of men to join his merry throng. It was in these days that his band grew to its strength of seven score great fighters, each of them a match for two ordinary men, and from then onward Robin was called the king of Sherwood.

But both Abbot Hugo and Isambart de Belame swore vengeance and waited their time. Robin, when he heard it, smiled.

"They are great swearers," he said.

How Robin Took Toll in Sherwood

CHAPTER VII

he tale of Guy of Gisbourne and his men returning in their shirts was still new when Robin and his men, out one morning on the track which ran from Mansfield to Nottingham, spied a party coming down the road, with a knight and a good dozen armed men in attendance on the rest of the travellers. For, since Robin had taken to the woods, men were shy of travelling even on the edge of Sherwood, unless in such companies as would give protection to the weak, or to those who carried goods worth the outlaw's attention. Here were two prosperous-looking merchants, who had evidently sought the protection of the knight and his men.

"Here is fair game for us," said Robin when he saw the party. "Do you, Little John, remain here with twenty men till they have passed you, and I will go on and stop them before they come to the bend."

They were all riding easily, the knight with his visor up and his lance held down, when a tall figure stepped out into the middle of the rutted track, and kneeling before them, with bow and arrow ready, bade them halt. It was Robin himself, and his men lined the track on either side of the way.

With a cry of dismay, the merchants and their followers and the men-at-arms came to a standstill, but the knight was made of different stuff. He dropped his visor, raised his lance, and, clapping in his spurs, thundered down on Robin, secure in his armour of proof, as he thought.

Now Robin, though he wore no armour, dropped his bow and drew his sword. The knight drove at him, reckoning on easy prey, but as he came Robin skipped aside and gave the horse a great blow on its nose with the flat of his hand. At that, as he had anticipated, the horse went rearing up on its hind legs and, with the shaken knight tugging at the reins, toppled over with a crash, leaving its rider senseless as it got to its feet and galloped away.

By that time the track was lined with archers, each with shaft fitted and ready to draw on any who resisted. One of the merchants was already on his knees beside the track, vowing candles to every saint he could think of, if only they would deliver him from these fierce outlaws.

"Down with your arms!" cried Robin to the men-at-arms, "or die!"

Outnumbered six to one or more, they had no choice. They were tied to each other and ranged alongside the track, while the mules on which the merchants' goods were carried underwent examination at the hands of Robin's merry men.

"Rich cloth of Lincoln green!" cried Much.

"And here is a pair of great silver candlesticks wrapped in the cloth."

"Good outlaw, spare me the candlesticks," begged the older and fatter of the merchants. "They are for the wife of the Sheriff of Nottingham, and he will flay me if I come to him without them."

"You would be none the worse for the loss of a layer or two of fat," Robin answered. "Still, if you will redeem the candlesticks, you may have them at ten gold marks for the pair."

"Ten gold marks?" the merchant echoed, aghast. "I have no more than that sum in my saddle bags."

"So!" said Robin calmly. He turned to the other merchant. "Good chapman," he said, "how much money do you carry?"

"But fifteen gold marks in all," said the merchant. "The rest I have expended in these goods I carry."

Robin turned to his men. "Little John, and you Scarlett, search the pair of them and let us see," he ordered.

So they searched, and found that the one who had confessed to fifteen marks had spoken the truth, but the one who claimed he had but ten was relieved of forty golden coins, which Little John held out to Robin.

"Keep it," said Robin, "and put it in our treasury. Take with it his silver candlesticks, for the man is a sorry liar. And tie him on his mule and drub him

down the road, for we will have no liars among us. But this other, give him
back his fifteen marks, and this day he shall dine with us, after which we will set
him on his way with all his goods untouched."

"Robin," cried Much from among the trees, "the knight has come to his
senses, and promises me a hanging."

"Tie his hands and let us take him with us," Robin ordered, "for he is an
ungentle knight, and I may give him a lesson in courtesy."

When the men-at-arms had been stripped of all their weapons and
armour and sent down the road, and the lying merchant had been bound on
his mule and soundly thwacked by Little John while he jolted after them,
Robin turned to the younger merchant, who stood by wondering.

"Now, sir," said Robin, "this day you shall dine with us, and over our
dinner we will settle what you pay as your footing among us. Bring that knight
along, Much, and let us away."

He led the wondering merchant into the forest, through glade and glen and
among great aisles of oaks that were old when Hastings field was fought over, until
they came to a wide, deep-set valley, to which access could only be gained by a winding path down the side of a steep cliff. Down in the valley were stout log huts set
along the banks of a clear stream; at the far end were butts
set up for the practice of archery, and, as they went down
the path, the merchant could see openings that
led into caves, in one of which a light burning
showed that men lived within.

"Truly, a wondrous stronghold,
outlaw," said the merchant, "and hard to
come at, I think."

"The ways are open," Robin answered,
"but I have only to blow a certain blast on this
horn I carry, and they will be closed in such
a way that you might search for a year and
never find this place, big though it is. And
the knight, you may see, is blindfolded."

Looking round, the merchant saw that this
was indeed so. And now Robin blew one short blast
on his horn, at which a couple of score men came
out from the huts in the valley to welcome their
chief and see what he had brought them. There was
a brave smell of cooking on the air, and the
merchant sniffed at it hungrily.

"Now," he said, "if I were but sure of my goods, I should have the heart to eat a right good meal here."

"Sure?" Robin echoed threateningly. "What mean you, merchant, by your 'sure'? Robin Hood has given you his word that your goods and your money shall go untouched, and no man who knows me doubts my word."

"Yet Robin Hood himself told me that I must pay my footing," the merchant reminded him.

Robin laughed at that. "A trifle—a mere trifle," he said. "We have forty gold marks and a rare haul of rich goods, to say nothing of a fine pair of silver candlesticks, for our day's haul, so we may deal lightly with an honest merchant who tells the truth."

"I pray you do," said the merchant, not yet quite reassured.

Robin turned about. "You may unblind that knight, Much," he said, "and ask him if he will dine with us."

"I will eat nothing with rogues and footpads," said the knight haughtily.

"Give me my sword and free my arms, and I will prove myself on any one of you."

"So much more good food for the rest of us," Robin said calmly. "Take off his blinkers, good Much, and strip that iron pot off his head and tie him to a tree, but downwind from our table, so that he may get the smell of the good food while we eat."

This was done, while the men in the valley fetched out great planks which they laid on trestles, and brought forth roast haunches of venison, and loins of wild boar, and hares and pheasants, all smoking hot, with good white bread and flagons of ale and wine, as fine a meal as the merchant had ever seen set out. He gazed in amazement at their stores.

"It is a table fit for a king," he said.

"It is a king's table," Robin answered, "for I am king in Sherwood, and these are my loyal subjects who eat with me. Now do you eat heartily, man, being our guest."

So the merchant fell to with a will, and made a right good meal with the outlaws, while next to him Little John ate so much that he cleared off everything within reach, though he did not forget to see that the guest had a good share too.

"Now," said Little John, having eaten twice as much as any other, "after that little snack I must e'en starve till supper. 'Tis a hard life, mine, wherever I feed."

Robin pushed a great flagon of ale toward the giant. "Wash down the little snack, John, and begin again," he offered.

But Little John shook his head. "Not so, Robin, for my appetite is in poor state to-day."

"In poor state?" the merchant echoed. "Man, never in my life have I seen any man stow away so much at a sitting, excepting only the hermit friar of Kirklees."

"I have heard tell of that friar," Robin said. "What sort of man is he, good merchant?"

"A mighty feeder, and they say a jovial soul," answered the merchant. "I have heard they made him fast too much in Kirklees, so he turned hermit, and now feeds as he will. Up the stream that runs past St. Mary's Abbey you will find the good friar, in all likelihood fishing, for he can both catch and cook a salmon skillfully. And I have heard he is not above tucking up his robe and going out after deer with his bow, on moonlit nights."

"O, a rare hermit!" said Robin. "A hermit above all price. And we have need of the ministrations of the Church in our band at times. I must find this hermit and persuade him to forgo his loneliness.

"I will go and see him when I have nothing better to do. If he dislike fasting and penances, he is a man after my own heart."

"But now," said the merchant, "what footing shall I pay for this meal of mine, good prince of merry outlaws?"

"This," said Robin. "When next you go toward Mansfield, you shall go out of your way to pay a visit to old Much, the miller there, and tell him his son is safe and happy in my band, also that young Much is not so lazy as he used to be."

"A light payment," said the merchant, "and I promise faithfully to go there within the week."

"But that is not all," Robin said. "For when you get to Much the miller, you will find that he has care of a young lad, Waltheof by name. You shall take for this lad a choice suit, all of Lincoln green, with shoes and cap as well, and give them to him without payment, for I have a kindness toward the boy."

"Right gladly will I do that too," the merchant promised.

"Then that is the footing for the meal," Robin said. "Now, since we have all eaten, we will see how the evil-tempered knight fares."

He led the way to the tree where Much had bound the knight, who glared at him as he came, but said no word.

He was a smallish, pale man, of a Norman cast of face, with little, deep-set eyes and thin lips. It was a cruel face that looked on the outlaws as they came to where he stood bound.

"What do they name you, knight?" Robin asked.

"I hold no speech with rogues," the knight answered shortly.

Robin turned to the merchant. "Good sir," he said, "what is the name of this Norman vermin?"

"He is called Roger de Gran," the merchant answered.

"Aye," Robin nodded, "I might have known it from his face—Roger the Cruel, one of Isambart de Belame's crew in Evil Hold. He it was who put out the eyes of two serfs with his own hand, because they took a hare on Belame's land, and there was a tale of a murdered woman—"

"A true tale," said Much, the miller's son. "She was wife to a man who had served my father in his time. This Roger killed her."

Robin gazed at the bound knight thoughtfully. "And he counted on riding me down, in armour and on a horse, against me with no armour and but a sword for my defence. Unknightly that, for though in the press of battle a man may strike how he will, yet in single combat there should be equality between man and man for a fight. Now what say you, Little John, shall we hang him?"

"You dare not hang a belted knight," Roger said scornfully.

"Dare not?" Robin echoed with wrath. "Why, you Norman hog, you disgrace to your gilt spurs, no man says 'dare not' to Robin Hood in Sherwood and goes free of his words. Here, Much, and you, Scarlett, untie this Norman carrion and strip him of his armour. And do you, Little John, get us four stout men to hold him, and bid two others cut good willow wands."

When all this had been done, and four men held Roger the Cruel, stripped to his underclothing, Robin pointed to the path out from the glade.

"We will not foul our home by hanging you here, Roger," he said, "but these four men shall lead you, blindfolded, back to the edge of Sherwood, and two more shall follow with the willow staves. For every tenth step you take, till you get to the edge of the forest, one of the staves shall be laid on your back— and see that you lay on hard, you two! It is time you robbers and oppressors of the poor had a taste of the goods you hand to them, and I will make a beginning now. Lead him away."

Then he turned to the merchant, who had watched this scene with awe, for it was beyond thinking that any knight, no matter how evil he might be, should be subjected to such disgrace.

"Friend," said Robin, "you have dined well and seen some of our justice, and now you will wish to get on your way. At the edge of the forest all your goods will be restored to you untouched, for we have no quarrel with honest men."

Then he bade a kindly farewell to the merchant, and gave him men to conduct him to the edge of the forest, where all his goods were waiting untouched, as Robin had promised. And when Little John had roared out what he thought was a song, and Much and Will Scarlett had had a bout of quarter-staff play to keep their hands in, the outlaws slept in their glade well-fed and content.

59

"Ho, you!" he said roughly. "Up and carry me across this stream, lest I wet my feet in the water."

"Son," said the friar gravely, not a bit discomposed in spite of the sword, "my dinner is here on this side. Why should I cross to the other?"

"Up and carry me!" Robin insisted. "Put down the dinner till I am over the ford dry-footed."

The friar put down his half-eaten pasty and sighed. "Since it must be, it must be," he said. "Get up on my back then."

He bent his back, and Robin got on it, but took care to keep his drawn sword in his hand. The friar took to the water and waded in.

"These be sad days," he lamented, "when a peaceful man must leave his dinner for any knave who fears to wet his feet."

He splashed on, with the water nearly waist deep in the middle of the ford, and came out on the other bank. Then, as Robin slipped from his back, the friar turned and gripped him with surprising agility, snatched away his sword, and flung him down on the turf.

"My turn to ride!" he said. "Up, man, and carry me back to my dinner, else I will spit you on this skewer of yours!"

There was no help for it, Robin knew—his own trick had been turned against him. He bent his back, and the friar, getting up on it, made him grunt with his great weight.

"Go carefully, man," he bade. "I can see that dinner of mine waiting there, and my mouth waters to finish it. In you go!"

Hidden in the bushes on the far bank, both Scarlett and Little John shook with laughter to see their chief take to the water with the mountain of a friar perched grinning on his back.

But when they got to the bank again, and the friar got down ponderously, Robin suddenly bent himself and jumped backward, hitting the friar in a way that knocked all the wind out of him and caused him to drop the sword. With a nimble leap Robin picked it up.

"No dinner yet, friar," he said. "Carry me back, and be careful over it, or I'll slice an ear off you."

Again the friar bent his back, since there was no help for it, but this time he looked none too pleasant. He took to the water, with Robin on his back, and waded in; when he had got to the middle he suddenly bent nearly double and pitched Robin into the stream over his head.

"Now, impudent rascal, sink or swim," he said. "I am for my dinner."

And back he went, leaving Robin to climb out from the water, laughing at the adventure. Presently Robin came up to him, with his sword in its sheath, all dripping from the water.

"Away, villain," said the friar, "or I will take a stick and baste your hide for you. Let me eat in peace."

"A bold monk this," said Robin. "Tell me your name."

"Men call me Friar Tuck. How do they call you, rascal?"

"Robin of Locksley, but better known as Robin Hood."

The friar leaped to his feet with a laugh. "What?" he asked. "Have I made carry me the man who sent Guy of Gisbourne home in his shirt and spoiled the rascally Prior of Newark?"

"So," said Robin, "but I made you carry me, too. Now, friar, there is more meat like that you are eating in Sherwood, and many a drink like that in your flask. I have come out to-day to find you."

"Here is a man who likes priors and abbots as little as I like them myself," said the friar, "and has as little respect for the King's deer as I have. But perhaps, Robin, you keep fast days in Sherwood. Is it so?"

"If you will join my band, we will keep just so many fast days as you order us," Robin promised.

"Ah, tempt me not, Robin Hood—tempt me not! For I am a holy man."

"Venison, friar—good fat deer, well cooked, a roast swan once in a while, and pheasants. Strong ale a-plenty, and good casks of wine as well. Come with us, for we need such a cook as I have heard you are."

"Enough, Robin—I yield," the friar said with a chuckle. "It is too much for sinful man to resist."

"Now we shall have a chaplain to our band," Robin remarked, and raised his hand in a signal, at which Scarlett and Little John came out of the wood toward their chief. Friar Tuck stared at the mighty form of Little John and sighed.

"Good Robin," he said, "if you keep such tiny babies in your band as this we must e'en take back some feeding bottles with us."

"If it were not for your robe and cowl, friar," said Little John, "I would cut me a quarter-staff and tan your hide for that saying."

"Cut it, man, and I will throw back the cowl and tuck up the robe," the friar offered. "For so they call me Friar Tuck, since ever my robe is tucked in my belt to let me fight more freely. Let us have a bout, and I will warrant you cry for mercy before it is over."

"We will have that bout in our glade, not here," said Robin. "Let us away, friar, if you are ready."

So Robin Hood won Friar Tuck to join his band, and they say there was no merrier or braver man than the good friar in all the Midlands. He could sing them a song, cook them a royal feast and fight well at need.

How Robin Won the Silver Arrow

CHAPTER IX

 ow that Robin had got his band together, little passed in the North Midlands, or in Yorkshire itself, of which he did not know, for the country people, seeing that he was for their rights and against the oppression of the barons and the church dignitaries, gave him and his men any aid they asked. This was the time when John ruled England in his brother's absence, and Queen Berengaria, together with the Queen-Mother, Eleanor, laid all England under heavy tribute to get together the money to ransom King Richard, who lay a prisoner to Luitpold of Austria in the castle of Gratz.

Even John himself, much as he feared his brother's return, helped to gather in tribute for the ransom, and for that purpose made a progress of the midland counties. When he came to Nottingham, the Sheriff, Robert de Rainault, held a tournament in his honour, for Robert was John's man and profited by John's tyrannies. Much, the miller's son, who had been to visit his father, brought back news of the tournament at the same time that he brought word to Robin of the boy Waltheof's new suit.

"The lad is a fine young cock now," said Much. "Prancing round in his Lincoln green, with a toy bow, and vowing that he will be Robin Hood's man when he is grown. Right well has the merchant fitted him out."

"I am glad the man was honest," Robin commented. "But what of this tournament in Nottingham, good Much?"

"They will hold it in Pike's field, under the wall of the town on the north side," Much announced. "Already, my father tells me, the lists are set for the knights, and the barriers raised, and now they make a great platform on which John is to sit with the Sheriff to watch the jousting of the knights and the contests between the men-at-arms. Two days of jousting, they say, and a day for the sports of the common people."

"So ever," said Robin, "two to the Norman thieves, and one to the people they rob, under John."

"But there will be rare sport on the third day," said Much, "for there is to be archery at a mark, after the sword-play on foot, and the prize for the best archer is a silver bugle and a silver arrow feathered with gold."

"A good prize," said Robin thoughtfully, "and I count that the Sheriff's man Hubert will hope to win it."

"He is afraid of one of the men who comes with Count John," said Much, "a leary fellow with a squint they call Henry—"

"Do they call the fellow Henry, or the squint, Much?" interrupted Little John, who was listening.

"Nay, but a pest on thy jokes," said Much, amid laughter. "This Henry is a mighty archer, they say, and will put a shaft in the clout at half a mile if there be no wind—"

"Given two good pots of ale, he would call it a mile," said Friar Tuck, "and for a third pot would make it from Nottingham to Sheffield."

"I have a mind to hang that bugle over my shoulder and to put the silver arrow in my quiver," said Robin Hood thoughtfully.

"There is too much risk in it, good master," Little John warned him. "Many a man in Nottingham would be glad of the forty gold marks the Sheriff set as the price of your head."

"And many a man there would guard me from the Sheriff," said Robin. "Little John, we will go after that bugle and the arrow. Out of all the clothes and armour we have taken of late, there will be disguises for a couple of score of us, and I will shoot for the Sheriff's prize."

They planned it out, decided who should go to Nottingham to see Robin shoot for the Sheriff's prize, and how they should disguise themselves.

When the day came, there arrived at Pike's field certain millers, dusty with the meal and flour of their trade, and cattle herders with smocks and hats pulled down over their eyes, and a giant beggar who limped on a crutch, as Little John had decided that was his best disguise, and all these watched the long-staff bouts and cheered the winners most lustily.

Although it was the third day of the tournament there was a brilliant gathering of knights and their ladies up in the stand with Count John and the Sheriff, and the field was thronged with sightseers from miles round, for seldom did such great people come to Nottingham. When the swordsmen had finished and the targets were set up for archery, the people flocked to the barriers on either side to see the shooting, as nearly sixty tall fellows stood forth to shoot.

Among them was an old, ragged man with dirty face and torn cap, who wanted to give in his name with the rest to the clerk who entered up the competitors. The clerk looked at him in doubt.

"'Tis a good bow, but I doubt if such a scarecrow as you have the strength to draw it," said the clerk. "Still, they will beat you in the first round. What name do you go by?"

"Men call me Hodden o' Barnsdale," the ancient quavered weakly, and wiped his eyes on his sleeve. "And I tell you, master clerk, I be as good as they young sprigs wi' a bow, for all your saying."

"Bragging ne'er sped an arrow yet, Hodden o' Barnsdale," said the clerk shortly, "and if you have tramped here from Barnsdale in Yorkshire you will have no strength left for shooting. Still, take your place, man."

Now Prince John, seeing this ragged ancient among so many stout fellows, leaned forward in his seat and called down to the lists.

"Clerk," he asked harshly, "what does that ragged beggar among the archers? Why is he there?"

"Sire," the clerk called back, "he enters himself to shoot against them for the silver bugle and arrow."

There was a ripple of laughter among the crowd, but the old man shook his fist at the clerk and turned to the royal stand.

"Your worship," he squeaked, "I be Hodden o' Barnsdale, and as good a man as these beef-fed louts, any day."

"Turn him out, clerk," cried the Sheriff.

"Not so," said John, "but let the man shoot. And if he put not an arrow in the target he shall be drubbed out of the lists."

"Have no fear, your worship," squeaked the old man. "My arrows shall find the target. They be English arrows, as English as the one that found Red William's heart."

Now an allusion of this sort to the shooting of William Rufus was an insult to any Norman, and especially to the one who hoped to wear Red William's crown. John leaned forward again, his face dark with anger.

"Mark that man, clerk!" he cried. "If he be not in the last dozen contestants, bring him before me to be whipped for a Saxon braggart."

There were many Saxons lining the lists that day, and they murmured openly at the insult, especially the tall beggar with the crutch. But now the archers were lined up, six at a time, for the first trial, which would leave one man in every six to shoot off for the prize. When Hodden o' Barnsdale's turn came, he was three inches nearer the centre of the target than any other of his six.

"Chance, mere chance," said the clerk angrily, for he had hoped to see old Hodden beaten.

There were now twelve men left, of whom the Sheriff's man Hubert had so far shot the best arrow, while Henry, the man of John's following, was next best—for though old Hodden had shot better than either, it was regarded as a chance shot. Now a single great target was set up, into which each man of the dozen must shoot an arrow in turn till each had shot three arrows, but if any

71

man missed the target altogether he must retire from the contest. The distance was one hundred and twenty yards.

The first two archers missed altogether, and walked off with mortification on their faces. Then came Hubert, who landed his shaft within six inches of the black spot in the centre of the target, and two more who only scored on the outer edge. Then old Hodden, stepping into place with a grin, loosed off a shaft so carelessly that he seemed to take no aim at all, and turned away before the arrow struck the target.

"Child's play, this," he said.

But from the watchers near the target a roar went up, for his arrow was in the black spot, which was barely half an inch across. Hubert stared hard at the old man.

"Does the devil ride your arrows, old fool?" he asked viciously.

"Nay," said old Hodden, "the devil fights shy of English arrows, as do you Normans."

Hubert rushed at him to strike him, but a couple of his fellows held him back. "Why spoil your aim?" they asked. "The old fool is not worth a blow. The shot was sheer luck, for he took no aim."

Then another roar went up, for Henry, John's archer, had planted a shaft within an eighth of an inch of old Hodden's. Hubert glared at the man angrily, and waited to see what the rest would do.

But no other archer came near the centre of the target in this first round, and, since three more missed altogether, there were but seven left for the second stage of the contest. Old Hodden, having made the best shot before, was set to shoot first when the fresh target was put up, and he loosed off his arrow with as little care as before.

"They should set up a mark to make it worth a man's while to try," he said as he turned away. "Shooting at that great white thing is no more than throwing stones in a pond."

And down at the other end of the range the spectators yelled and threw up their hats. "To Hodden—to Hodden!" they cried, for the old man had put his arrow in the black spot again. But when John's man Henry had shot they went wild, for Henry split Hodden's arrow with his shot.

"Man," said Hodden to Henry, "there are few archers like us two, and be he Norman or English, I love a man who can put in such a shaft as that."

Henry regarded the old man curiously. "I would take a lesson or two off you, Master Hodden," he answered, "for mine is my best shooting, while with you it is a matter of ease."

"Later maybe," Hodden said. "Let us see what this braggart of the Sheriff's choosing will do."

But Hubert cursed when he saw that his shaft was a good two inches off the spot, though he had dwelt long on his aim. Still, he cheered up when two more of the seven missed this smaller target, and left only five for the final shot, with only Hodden and Henry better than himself.

Now the clerk, turning toward where John sat, called out the names of the five left in, and John signed to him.

"Bring them before us, clerk," he called.

So the five were ranged before the stand, with Henry on the right, and Hodden o' Barnsdale next to him. John nodded at his man.

"Go to it, Henry," he bade, "and when I hand you the bugle I will see that it is filled with silver pennies."

"Your worship," old Hodden squeaked, "he hath yet to win the prize. When I have beaten him, will the bugle be filled wi' silver pennies for me?"

"Ha! You beat Henry?" John mocked. "Aye, if you can beat such an archer as he I will surely fill the bugle with silver pennies."

"Thank ye, your worship. Since a Norman thief stole my land my old woman ha' wanted a new gown, and the pennies 'ull buy her a rare one."

"Aye," said John, angered again, "and you who dare call Normans thieves to our face shall have your right hand cut off when Henry has beaten you and taken the bugle. Away with them to their work, clerk, and watch this old rascal closely, lest he run away after his shot."

The five were ranged up before a still smaller target, and Henry, being judged the best shot of the five after his last feat, was first to shoot. He missed the black spot in the centre by a bare half inch and stood back with a frown of vexation. Then old Hodden raised another cheer as he planted his arrow in the black, but not exactly in the centre. Then came Hubert, the Sheriff's man, whose arrow struck level with old Hodden's in the black, so that the two shots were exactly equal. The other two made worse shots than Henry, and retired.

"Your worship," said the clerk to the Sheriff, "Hubert and Hodden o' Barnsdale must shoot it off, for they have tied for first place."

"If they are to shoot it off," said John, as he sat beside the Sheriff, "then my man Henry must shoot too, for it was but by chance that he missed the black this time."

It was dead against all rules, as everyone knew, but the heir to the throne was not to be contradicted. So a fourth target was set up at a hundred and fifty yards, and Hubert, whose shot in the last round was reckoned the best, shot first—and missed the target altogether!

"A trick of the wind—a trick of the wind!" the Sheriff cried. "Let him shoot again!"

73

"Let him stand down," John growled, fearful lest his man should be beaten. "One shot and no more. Do you shoot now, Henry."

So, though by the rules of the game it was old Hodden's turn, Henry stood forward, dwelt long on his aim, and shot. There was a buzz of applause, for his arrow landed in the black, though well to the left.

"Now, old fool!" John cried, excited over his man's shooting, "take your stand and loose your last arrow, before you lose your hand."

With no sign of fear, Hodden stepped to his place, and this time, it was noted, he took more careful aim. The great arrow hummed from the string and struck with a thud, and again the crowd roared applause, for Hodden's shot had split Henry's arrow, and landed in the centre of the black. Old Hodden nodded and grinned.

"Now how many silver pennies go to fill a bugle?" he asked.

John leaped up from his place and walked down to the target, inspecting it narrowly. Then he came back.

"It is a tie," he declared. "They must shoot it off." For still he hoped to see his man win, and cheated thus in his decision to make another chance for Henry.

"Dread lord," said Henry, "what shall we shoot at? For unless the wind trick us, and the day is still with no wind, we shall never decide."

"Your worship," said old Hodden, "this shooting at walls o' white is but a game for babes. Let us set up a peeled willow wand at a hundred and fifty cloth yards, and the first to split it takes the bugle."

"Why then, you old fool," said John, "we shall sit here till Christmas and longer, for no man ever hit such a target."

"Lord," said Henry, "I have heard of such shooting, and once I have hit such a target, though but at fifty yards. If the old man is willing, then so am I."

"So be it," said John. "One shot apiece, and he who shoots nearest to the wand shall take the bugle and the silver arrow."

The last target was cleared away, a slip of willow peeled and stuck in the ground, and the distance carefully measured off.

"Do you shoot first," Hodden said to his opponent, "for there are clouds coming over the sun, and I would give you the best light."

"Master," said Henry, "you be a right courteous old man, and I thank you. But no man can hit the wand at that distance, and we must find another mark when we have failed at this."

He made a good attempt, dwelling long on his aim, and twice lowering his bow at the merest breath of wind. At last he shot, and a great "Ooh!" of wonder went up from the watchers, for his arrow had grazed the wand.

"A fine shot, good Henry," said old Hodden, as he stooped and plucked a spike of grass. He threw it in the air, to get the set of the faint breeze, twanged his bowstring, and set the arrow on it. Then he stepped to the mark, took careful aim, and let fly. A mighty shout went up when it was seen that he had split the wand fairly with the arrow.

"This is not a man—it is a demon in human form," said John.

"Demon or man, lord, he hath won the prize," the Sheriff reminded him.

Old Hodden turned to Henry and held out his hand. "Though the bugle is mine, do you take the pennies out of it, Master Henry," he said, "for I would not wish to shoot against a better man."

But Henry shook his head. "I have pennies a-plenty, old man," he answered, "and the full prize is yours, fairly won. Do you take it all, and may we yet meet for another match."

"I trust so," said Hodden. "I will now go and claim my prize."

So he went up to where John, very unwillingly, held the silver bugle full of pennies in one hand, and the beautiful gold and silver arrow in the other. John frowned at him fiercely.

"Old man," he said, "I would I had had that right hand of yours lopped off rather than you should take this prize. Take it and begone."

"For such courtesy, your worship, no less than for the prize, my thanks," Hodden answered, and took the bugle and the arrow. With a quick movement he swung the bugle, flinging its contents of silver pennies far and wide among the people who stood round to watch, and then he backed away from where John and the Sheriff sat.

"Stop—hold that man!" John cried out. "'Tis some thief disguised, for such as he seems do not fling silver pennies away."

But Hodden was already clear of the crowd about the stand, and, with an arrow ready on his string, he pointed straight at John's craven heart.

"Take back that order, or die, Count John!" he cried in ringing tones.

"Let him go—let him go!" John yelled, in sheer terror.

Now Guy of Gisbourne, who had watched the shooting, and more especially had kept an eye on old Hodden, suddenly reached out and grasped the archer's tattered old hat. It came off, and with it the dirty old grey wig and beard that had concealed his face.

"'Tis Robin Hood—seize him!" Guy shouted. "Outlawed—forty marks for the man who takes him—"

But he said no more, for just then the limping beggar raised his crutch and brought it down on Guy's head with such force that he dropped senseless, and Little John's voice roared out:

"To Hood! To Hood! To us, merry men, English all!"

A score or more of stout fellows, armed with great quarter-staves, came knocking their way through the crowd that gathered round, and Robin, seizing a staff, retreated with them after he had slung his bow so as to have both hands free. Meanwhile Little John's shout had served its purpose of setting the Saxon English people of Nottingham against John's Norman followers, and in five minutes or less there were a dozen separate fights going on, while John and the Sheriff fled for safety, and Robin and his men retreated steadily beyond the barriers of the tournament grounds.

Here they came on a body of men-at-arms, set to keep order among the crowd, and now drawn up with swords ready to stop them. But Robin and Little John advanced with a rush, with quarter-staves whizzing round them, and the first who tried conclusions with them found their swords either shattered or whirled out of their hands by the flying staves. And when Will Scarlett, Much and the rest of the band joined issue with the men-at-arms, and the staves rattled on their pates in earnest, such as were not laid stunned took to their heels and bolted, while the good people of Nottingham roared with laughter to see John's hated followers put to flight in such fashion.

Without the loss of a man, Robin drew off, and the surging crowds prevented any men whom the Sheriff sent in pursuit from finding which way he had gone. The outlaws reached the shelter of the forest in safety, and made their way to their retreat.

"'Twas a joyous adventure, Robin," said Little John, as they ate together, "but we will not go to Nottingham again this month."

"No," said Robin, "unless they hold another shooting match. I would I had another crack at that man Henry, for he shoots a good arrow."

The Rescue of Maid Marian

CHAPTER X

~

bout a fortnight after the tournament at Nottingham, when Roger the Cruel's back had so far healed that he could go out again, and the Sheriff of Nottingham had proclaimed far and wide that he would give fifty marks to any man in return for Robin Hood's head, Isambart de Belame came to Hugo de Rainault, Abbot of St. Mary's. Hugo welcomed his ally in his own comfortable room in the Abbey, sent for a flagon of his best wine, and settled to hear what Isambart had to say.

"The summer is passing," said Isambart, "and I would get married before the crops are gathered, Abbot Hugo."

"A wise resolve," Hugo agreed, nodding. "So you come to me for a priest to marry you in the chapel of Belame?"

"A priest, yes," said Isambart, "and the bride as well, according to our bargain when I lent you thirty of my men to root out the outlaws from Sherwood Forest."

"Surely, man," the Abbot protested, "you would not claim that bargain?"

"A bargain is a bargain," Isambart retorted.

"But what came of it? The rascally outlaws spoiled my steward and his men of their armour and clothes, and sent them out to be a laughingstock, and Robin Hood is stronger than ever."

"Hugo," said Isambart, "it was agreed that if I lent you thirty men to follow Guy of Gisbourne, the maid Marian should be given to me. Now I claim her of you. I, too, have lost thirty good suits of my men's armour over that venture, and I tell you, Abbot, that a bargain is a bargain."

"Not this bargain," the Abbot insisted stubbornly.

Isambart got on his feet. "If you break your word with me, Hugo," he said, "we are friends no longer, and I will spoil your lands with the rest."

"Sit down, man," said Hugo, "and let us talk it over. Be not so hasty. You say you would wed the maid."

"That was the bargain," Isambart agreed, sitting down again.

"Ha! Hum!" Hugo reflected awhile, for he could not afford to break his friendship with Isambart. "Well," he said when he had thought it out, "the maid has no taste to be a nun, and she must marry somebody. I will send to Kirklees and bid her prepare to marry you."

"When?" Isambart asked, rather grimly.

"I will send a man to-morrow," the abbot promised.

"Now look you, Abbot," said Isambart, "this is no matter for shifts and tricks. Send your steward, Guy of Gisbourne, with an escort of a dozen good men, and have the maid convoyed safely to my castle of Belame within the week. Send me, too, a priest to marry us, and the bargain will then be kept. Shall it be so?"

Hugo nodded assent, reluctantly, for there was no way out of it that he could see. When Isambart had gone he sent for Guy of Gisbourne and explained what must be done.

"So you take the men, Guy, and set out tomorrow," he bade. "Have them all well mounted, and ride to Kirklees for the maid. And see that you go well armed, and keep clear of Robin Hood and his men till the maid is safely at the castle of Belame."

Guy flushed with anger, for he had no liking for reminders of the way Robin Hood had served him and his men in Sherwood. But he went out obediently enough to do the Abbot's bidding.

Next day came a wandering beggar into Robin Hood's retreat in Sherwood, one of the scouts who brought in news every day to the outlaws' hold, and he told how Guy of Gisbourne and his men were setting out to escort Marian from Kirklees.

"Aye," said Robin, "but where do they take her? Not to the Abbey, surely, for that is no place for her?"

"They take her to Castle Belame, to be married to Isambart, Robin."

"What?" Robin shouted. "Marry a fair maid to that thieving wolf? Is the maid willing, think you?"

"She knows naught of it," said the beggar. "Abbot Hugo made a bargain with Isambart over the loan of certain men for hunting you, and Isambart claims his price."

"Ah, the foul Norman thief!" said Robin in disgust. "Now I say this shall not be. One wife of Isambart's has pined to death in Evil Hold, and there shall be no more while I rule in Sherwood."

"Once she gets to Evil Hold," said Friar Tuck, who listened, "there is no rescuing her, Robin."

"She shall not get to Evil Hold," Robin answered. "Let us arm a couple of score of the band with the good armour we took from Guy of Gisbourne and his men, and ambush him on his way to Isambart's castle."

And so it was done. Robin sent out spies to find out the road by which Guy of Gisbourne would travel to Evil Hold, and, when the time came, set out with his men and lay up in a thicket beside the track, a little beyond Worksop. They had waited half a morning, and began to fear that Guy had taken some other road, when Robin spied a couple of armed men riding down from the Yorkshire border, and there was talk and the clatter of hoofs behind them. When they were still a score yards away he stood out alone in the middle of the

79

track, and saw Guy, heavily armed, leading a white palfrey on which rode the maid he had been sent to find at Kirklees and escort to Isambart's hold.

With an arrow on the string, Robin stood, and the two foremost men reined in at sight of him.

"Stand, Guy of Gisbourne!" Robin cried. "Deliver up the maid for safe escort back to Kirklees, and I will do you no harm."

They say that Marian, seeing him standing there, one man defying a score, loved him from that minute. For the journey had been a thing of dread for her, and she loathed the thought of going to Evil Hold, yet could see no way of escape, since she was Hugo's ward and must do his bidding. But Guy pointed at the lone figure with a yell.

"Robin Hood—seize him, men! Fifty gold marks wait for the man who takes him! At him, you villains!"

Now fifty gold marks, in those days, would buy a farm and leave some over, so Guy's men needed no second bidding. The two foremost spurred at him, one a little in front of his fellow, and Robin's arrow crashed into the brain of the leading horse, which, falling to earth, lay in the track so that the second rider came to grief. The two of them lay stunned and helpless, one pinned down by the dead horse and the other kicked by his floundering steed before it got up and galloped away.

"Must I be always baulked by this rascally hound?" Guy roared in rage. "At him, you others, and seize the outlaw!"

But not one of them moved to obey, for Robin had another arrow on the string, and they knew since the tournament at Nottingham that he never

80

missed. With a curse, Guy dropped the palfrey's rein, drew his sword, and spurred at the lone figure just as Robin raised his silver bugle and blew a blast on it. Suddenly the woods became alive with armed men, surrounding the maid and Guy's followers, while Robin stepped aside as his enemy thundered past, and stooped to evade the swish of the sword.

"Foul stroke, Guy," he said, as Guy tried to rein in and come back at him. "Get down, man, and let us have it out."

But Guy looked back and saw that his men were all being disarmed and pinioned by Robin's followers, who outnumbered his party by two to one and more. He struck in his spurs and galloped on, leaving Marian to her fate.

Robin watched the fleeing man for perhaps a hundred yards, and then lifted his bow. The heavy arrow sang on its way and took the horse behind his shoulder, so that he came down with a mighty crash, and Guy lay in his armour on the track. Robin strode up to him and prodded him with his foot, laughing.

"Why, man," he said, "this is a poor sort of escort. To leave a maid in distress, in the hands of savage outlaws, is no sort of play for an honest steward. How will it sound in the ears of Abbot Hugo when he hears?"

Guy scrambled to his feet. "Mocker and thief!" he said fiercely, "if I had but my sword you should mock no more."

Robin pointed to where the sword had fallen. "Take the sword," he said, "and though you be in armour and I but clad for the woods, we will try a bout here and now, steward. For surely you will strike a blow for the maid you were set to guard?"

The game was up, Guy knew. He could not hope to get Marian out of the clutches of Robin and his men, and, with his horse lying dead, there was no chance of flight.

"And if I beat you," he said sullenly, "your men will but kill me."

"Now, now!" Robin protested, "that is the way of a Norman cur, I know well, but it is not the way of us of the greenwood. Should you beat me, Guy of Gisbourne, you go free to your master, but the maid shall not go to Isambart in Evil Hold. So take your sword, and let us see if your work with it is as big as your bragging."

Without more ado Guy took up his sword, and found Robin ready when he turned to stand on guard. They went at their grim work with a will, and the flashing blades ground on each other as they thrust and parried, while Robin's men, having disarmed and tied up Guy's followers, came round to watch the duel, and Marian urged the palfrey forward with a prayer for the safety of her deliverer.

For ten minutes or more the blades flashed in the sunlight, and Guy panted in his armour, striving with every trick he knew to get past Robin's guard; but in vain. By the end of that time it was apparent that Robin was merely playing with his opponent, dancing round him and fencing lightly with a smile on his lips.

"Now steady, Guy," he bade mockingly. "Save breath, man—save breath! If the Abbot have no better swordsmen than you, his Abbey is poorly guarded. Bad thrust—try again!"

A little ripple of laughter went up from the watchers, which infuriated Guy. He made a couple of wild passes that Robin parried easily, and then with a twist so quick that no man could tell quite how it was done Robin ripped his sword out of his grasp and sent it flying into the bushes.

"Now, steward," he said, lowering his own point, "what shall we do with you? We have already one suit of your armour, and it would be a pity to spoil you of this you wear."

"Mock me no more," said Guy sullenly, "but kill me and make an end."

"This is no day for killing," Robin answered. "Get you gone to Abbot Hugo and tell him the maid is in safe keeping on her way back to Kirklees. Tell him, too, that if Isambart press his suit any more, I will come and burn Evil Hold about his ears."

"You mean to let me go?" Guy asked incredulously.

"Why should I keep you?" Robin answered. "It would but be wasting the food that a good man might eat, and we in Sherwood do not hunt the deer to feed such as you."

He turned and beckoned to Little John. "Turn these men of his loose, each with his hands so tied behind his back that they cannot untie each other," he said. "And tie Guy's hands too, and put him on a horse, for he is tired after that bout with the sword. Now do you, Guy, ride with these men where you will, so long as you ride away from here, and see that you do not come against me again, or I may not treat you so easily next time."

When Little John and the rest had done his bidding, Robin watched Guy and his sorry band of followers ride off toward St. Mary's Abbey. Then he turned to Marian, who still sat waiting on the white palfrey.

She was slim and fair, the chroniclers tell, with great blue eyes and hair of gold, a right fair maid, who, at her father's death, had been given into the wardship of Abbot Hugo till she should come of age and marry with his approval. Robin made her a low bow.

"We have saved you from the clutch of Isambart de Belame," he said, "and now, if you will, we will escort you back to safety at Kirklees."

"Good sir," she answered, "I have no wish to go back to Kirklees, for if I did I should still be at the mercy of Abbot Hugo, who perhaps would yet find a way to send me to the fiend who rules in Evil Hold."

"Why, that is true," said Robin, "yet a fair maid like you cannot wander about the world with nobody to guard and shelter you, and all your lands and wealth are in Hugo's clutches, I know. Where can you go, if not to Kirklees?"

Marian looked down and blushed. "I am among loyal, honest men, I see, in spite of the tales I have heard of Robin Hood and his men. May I not remain among them?"

Robin came near and looked into her eyes.

"It would give us all great joy to have such a one among us," he told her, "yet the greenwood is no place for maidens who have been used to shelter and every care. 'Tis but a rough life we live in the forest glades, and you would soon weary of it."

"Good Robin," she answered, "I had sooner have my freedom among good men, and go in rags, than live in luxury and know fear of those round me. Find me shelter, and when I come to my inheritance I will repay you."

"Nay, now," Robin said, "there is no question of repayment. What say you, Little John, shall we give her her will, and take such a fair flower as this to the shelter of the forest?"

Marian turned to Little John. "Good giant," she said, "plead for me with your chief. I have great knowledge of medicines and the art of healing, and I can cook and sew for you."

"Well, Robin," said Little John, "there is Will Scarlett's wife for company for her, and if, as she says, she have knowledge of medicines, she may find something that will sweeten Dame Scarlett's tongue, for it is bitter enough, and so poor Will may have an easier time."

"Think what it would have been for me if I had been taken to Evil Hold, good Robin Hood," Marian urged. "Is life in the greenwood any worse than such a fate as that?"

"If it were," Robin answered, "I would go and beg the Sheriff of Nottingham to hang me out of hand. I see no choice, Marian, for, as you say, if we take you back to Kirklees, Isambart will get you sooner or later, and there is no other place that would hold you now that Abbot Hugo has bidden that you be given up. But it is a poor fate for such a maid as you."

She looked down at him. "It is such a fate as I would ask," she said, "and I will come and be one of your band gladly. Now let us go on, lest Guy of Gisbourne rouse up more men to fight you."

Robin laughed. "If Guy's fighting is all we are likely to suffer from," he said, "life will be an easy business. You shall come and be queen of Sherwood, Marian—how say you, men? Will she not make a fair queen to rule over our band?"

Little John flung his hat in the air. "Here is a joyous adventure!" he cried. "Three cheers, all of you, for the queen of Sherwood!"

They roared their cheers so lustily that Abbot Hugo might have heard them at St. Mary's had he been listening. Robin reached up and grasped Marian's hand.

"Remember," he said, "that there is a king in Sherwood too, Marian. Would you be queen to me as well as to Sherwood?"

"Right gladly," she answered, "for I have seen no such man as you in all my life, and I owe you freedom and everything else from to-day."

Robin gave the word to move, and they set out on their way back to the forest hold. As they went Little John came up beside his leader, who rode by the white palfrey talking to Marian.

"Robin," said Little John, " 'Twas a lucky chance that sent you to win our friar to the band, for now he can do the marrying between you two, and we shall have no need to borrow a priest from St. Mary's."

"True," said Robin, "and we will make a feast day of it, and set the good friar to cooking after he has made us two man and wife."

So it was done, and they say that there was no such fair and loving wife in all the Midlands as was Maid Marian to Robin Hood. And, though he knew that he had made a bitter enemy of Isambart de Belame by this rescue, Robin slept none the worse for it.

Isambart, furious though he was, remembered how thirty men of his and twenty of the Abbot's had been sent out of Sherwood in their shirts, so he took no action for the time. But he waited for revenge all the same.

Abbot Hugo Pays Tribute

CHAPTER XI

hough Isambart de Belame was content to bide his time rather than attack Robin Hood at once, Abbot Hugo was in no such mind. He knew that Marian, when she came of age the next year, would be able to dispose of her lands and wealth as she would, and he had no mind to lose control of such an inheritance. One morning, attended only by a couple of friars, he set out early from St. Mary's to go to Nottingham and see what his brother the Sheriff, Robert de Rainault, could do to help him.

Usually, when he travelled, Abbot Hugo went in great state, with retainers of the Abbey to guard him and a score of his monks to attend his journey, but matters had come to such a pass along the rough tracks of the county now that he was afraid, if he went with any show at all, that Robin Hood would attack him. So he sneaked away while the day was young, hoping that Robin's scouts would fail to see him. But each of his friars bore, tied under his girdle, a great bag of gold marks with which to pay the men whom Abbot Hugo hoped to borrow from his brother the Sheriff, for hunting down Robin Hood and his band.

The forest glades looked fair and silent enough as the three of them, mounted on stout mules, rode toward Nottingham, and Abbot Hugo, feeling that with the Sheriff's aid he could make an end of the outlaw, was in high good humour. He joked and talked with his two attendants as mile after mile passed, his spirits rising as they drew near the end of their journey.

"Another hour," he said, "and I shall be able to rest with my good brother. These rough beasts make the bones ache."

"Aye, Lord Abbot," said Friar Anselm, "and a flagon of good Robert de Rainault's wine will be right welcome after such a ride."

He had barely spoken when his rein was seized by a man who darted out from the forest shades, and a dozen more surrounded the party.

"Saints preserve us! 'Tis those fierce outlaws!" the Abbot exclaimed. "Hold, fellows—we be of Holy Church, we three."

"Then is Holy Church so much the worse off, for three such scandalous villains never disgraced her before," said Robin Hood, stepping out from behind a tree. "Pull me that fat Abbot off his mule, Will Scarlett, and let us tie him to a tree and have a talk with him."

"But this is outrage—it is sacrilege!" the Abbot yelled.

"Just such outrage as when you would have sent a fair and innocent maid to the clutches of Isambart de Belame," Robin answered. "Pull him down, Will, and clout him over the ear if he resists."

But the Abbot came to ground without another word, while other men of the band helped the two friars to dismount.

"Good Robin," said Little John, "we have made a rare haul here. For this fellow hath a great fat bag under his gown, and there is a mighty pleasant clink in it."

"Dare to touch the bag, and you hang, all of you," the Abbot roared. "It is—it is tax for the King's ransom."

"Why, you fat liar," said Robin with a laugh, "one of my own men heard you say this morning that it was for your brother the Sheriff, to buy men to hunt me down."

"Robin!" yelled Much, who was searching the other friar, "this one hath a great bag of coin, too!"

"Verily," said the Abbot, with tears of vexation in his eyes, "it would need an army to make these forest tracks safe, even for such holy men as we."

"Empty the bags, and see how much his holiness was about to pay for our capture," Robin bade. "I trust he rates us at a fair price."

So, while the Abbot stood by, murmuring the maledictions of the Church on all outlaws, and his two friars prayed at a great rate, expecting to be killed in some murderous way, the money was counted into Little John's hat, which was big enough to hold it.

"Four hundred and fifty gold marks," said Little John, when all had been counted into the hat. "Never has my poor hat been so rich before."

"An insult, Abbot," said Robin, "for it rates my tall fellows at only three marks apiece, seeing that there are seven score of them."

"Ah!" said the Abbot, grinding his teeth, "you shall hang for this."

"Not so free with that tongue of yours, Abbot," Little John warned him, "or we may do a little hanging ourselves."

"You dare not lay hands on me, you sacrilegious rogue!" the Abbot retorted fiercely, for he had plenty of courage.

"We dare just as much as you dare with the wretched serfs under you, Abbot," Robin told him contemptuously. "And you dared to lie to us concerning this gold, so I tell you that it shall be put to the purpose you said. I will send it as Sherwood's share of the tax toward King Richard's ransom, from the king of Sherwood and his men. What say you, men?"

"A good use for the gold," said Little John. "Out of his revenues squeezed from his lands Abbot Hugo can find other gold for our hunting."

"What?" the Abbot cried, "do you steal my gold?"

Robin shook his head. "We do but put it to the use you said it was for," he answered. "If we can but get good King Richard back to England there may be an end to the oppressions of rogues like you."

"Do you dare insult me, villain?" the Abbot roared furiously.

"Now see here, scum of the Church," Robin answered quietly, "I have with me enough men to beat you to a jelly, if they only give a couple of blows apiece. So far the skins of all three of you are whole, but if you bandy words with us much longer they will be broken, for I will have you beaten with quarter-staves unless you get back on your mules and go about your business."

The Abbot looked as if he were about to reply, but thought better of it. He climbed back on to his mule, muttering, "Four hundred and fifty good gold marks!"

Robin laughed. "So shall we get our King Richard back the sooner," he said, "and you will rejoice, Abbot, that you helped to make up his ransom, when you think it over. Now away with you, all three, and leave the forest ways to decent people."

The three rode off, the two friars glad to escape so lightly, and Abbot Hugo in a rage at Robin for waylaying him, and at himself for hoping to escape the attention of the outlaws by travelling in such an undignified fashion. Now, he knew, he must go to Nottingham and meet his brother without a single piece of gold, and though he might promise payment for help, he knew well that Robert de Rainault, his brother, was not a man to set much store by promises.

Still, there was no help for it and he must do his best. He could get Robert to send an escort to St. Mary's to fetch more gold and thus make good his promises.

While he thought thus, Robin had the gold repacked in the two bags, and taken off to his hold. Four days later it was delivered to the King's justiciary at York, with a little slip of parchment which read:

> This tax of four hundred and fifty marks, collected in the Forest of Sherwood by me, Robin Hood, is hereby paid toward the ransom for our good King Richard, whom God preserve. And it is delivered by order of me, Robin Hood, to be used for this purpose and no other.

But the Abbot, when he came to his brother at Nottingham, was too angry to keep quiet over the way in which he had been trapped and made to yield up his gold. So the tale went about of how Robin had spoiled him, and many a man laughed to think that the fat Abbot had been made to give up some of his gains to help bring King Richard back to his throne again, when the very last man Abbot Hugo wanted to see in England was this same Richard, who had no love for such oppressors.

And when it got about that the Abbot had meant to use this money to pay for the capture of Robin Hood and his band, the laughter was great indeed. For very few people had sympathy with Abbot Hugo, since everyone knew his character as a grasping and cruel man, while many had sympathy with Robin Hood, whose generosity and courage were known to all.

The Taking of Will Scarlett

CHAPTER XII

~

inter came and passed, and summer returned to clothe Sherwood in green, and Robin and his band flourished, while men said that King Richard was on his way back to England after his captivity. The outlaws hunted the deer and lived right royally, and even in the depth of winter Marian declared that she had never lived so happily as in the forest. From time to time Robin and his men made a haul from some band of Normans who passed along the forest ways, or spoiled some fat prelate of the gains he had squeezed from his unfortunate tenants, and no man dared to oppose him after the discomfiture of the Guy of Gisbourne and his men when they went to seize the outlaw chief.

Robin was careful that his men were kept busy over something, for he knew that idleness breeds discontent more surely than anything else. When the weather was open there was hunting in the forest, and if they were forced to keep at home in their secret glade there were bouts of arms, archery contests, and grappling, at which both Much and Little John were mighty players, beating even Robin Hood himself, though he too was skilled at wrestling.

On a June day the good friar and Little John had a set-to at quarter-staves, a mighty battle that raged for nearly half an hour without advantage to either, though both got in many a hearty blow. They rested on their staves at last, both winded and hot from their exertions.

"A little more beef in that arm of yours, baby John," said the friar, "and you would make a rare fighter."

"And a little less strong ale with your venison, Friar Tuck, would give you more wind to stand up against me."

"Wind?" said the good friar. "Guard your head again for that, baby, for I have a-plenty wind left to blow it off, if I do not crack it with my staff first."

With a laugh, Little John went to it again, and the humming staves clashed and swung as each man tried his best. But suddenly Friar Tuck drew back, and pointed at a man running down the hillside into the glade.

"Hold, John!" he bade, "for that is Much, hurrying back to us. And never have I seen Much hurry before—there must be something wrong."

"Robin! Robin!" Little John called, and Robin Hood came out to see what the shouting was about.

In a few minutes Much told his tale, the end of which he had got from a serf of Isambart's, who had heard the baron say that Isambart de Belame hath captured Will Scarlett, and will hang him at the next noon outside his castle gate, as an example to all outlaws.

"Not while there is a man in Sherwood," said Robin grimly. "Let us get together and make a plan, for we will teach a lesson to the lord of Evil Hold for daring to meddle with a man of mine."

Swiftly the leaders of the band were got together for a council, for they knew well that Evil Hold was a very strong place, and the rescue of Scarlett could only be accomplished with great difficulty. But Robin was determined to get his man back, if he had to besiege the place.

"Yet I fear this is no matter for siege," he said, "for we should lose half our band if we set about it in that fashion. We have no engines to batter down great stone walls."

"Good Robin," said Much, "there is a man of our band, a mason, who helped in the building of Evil Hold when he was a lad. Let us get him up and see if he knows aught of a way in."

"A way in is easy enough," Robin answered, "but 'tis a way out that we need. Still, let us hear what this man says."

So Much found the man, a burly fellow who was a better hand with his sword than with a long bow, and who was named Dickon of Hartshead, since that was the village where he was born.

"Now, Dickon," said Robin, "what can you tell us of the make of Isambart's castle, and if there is any way by which a man may get in and out from it again."

"Master Robin, there is a way," Dickon answered. "It is a postern gate of iron, strong as the wall itself, set at the back of the castle from the great central gate. Isambart had it built there and masked by a deep arch, as a way to take out corpses so that none might see them when he had done any murders. At least, so they said when I helped build the walls of Evil Hold with the rest."

"And can a man get in by that postern?" Robin inquired thoughtfully.

Dickon shook his head. "No more than he may go through the wall itself," he answered, "for it is an iron gate, and very strong. But a man inside might get out by it unseen—I know no other way."

"Then," said Robin, "I will go in at Evil Hold by the main gateway, and come out with Will Scarlett by the postern. Do you instruct me all you know of the inner ways of Evil Hold, Dickon, while Little John and our good friar warn the men of the band that we march an hour before dawn, in forest gear and with bows, but not in armour."

"Not in armour, son Robin?" Friar Tuck queried in surprise. "But all Isambart's men will be heavily armed. How shall we fight them?"

"Sit about in groups outside, out of reach of their crossbow bolts, and shoot at every head that shows—our long bows can outshoot them by five score yards," Robin explained. "When they see you all unarmoured, I hope Isambart will set his men on you, and then, if you run for the forest in time, not a man shall we lose. While this sham attack goes on, leave it to me to find Will Scarlett and bring him out."

"Or else we lose you too, and then we are all lost men," said Little John. "Let some other go inside, Robin."

"Not so," Robin rejoined. "I will bring him out. Now let us to it, good Dickon, for I need to know every passage and door of which you can tell me inside that place."

Dickon took a stick and drew plans on the ground with it till dark, while Robin questioned him closely, until from central keep and the dungeons under it to the outer walls the outlaw chief knew all that his man could tell him of the inner ways of Evil Hold. After that, the outlaws slept till Friar Tuck roused them two hours before dawn, when they found Robin already up and waiting.

"But how will you get into Evil Hold?" Little John asked. "Isambart would as soon hang you as look at you."

"Leave that to me," said Robin.

With him he had two great bundles that looked like baskets tied up in sacks, and when Little John wanted to know what they were he shook his head and smiled.

"That is my army," he said. "With it I will put to flight every man of Isambart's, if there be need."

"A mad venture, I fear," said Friar Tuck, shaking his head. "I fear lest we lose you, Robin."

"Mad or not, it shall succeed," Robin answered, "else is our good Will Scarlett a dead man. Now march, men, for it is time."

They set off, and after four hours' hard tramping came to where the forest gave way to the open lands around the hill on which stood Evil Hold, Isambart's great castle from which he ruled harshly over all the country round, levying tribute on the peaceful villagers till they were half starved between his exactions and those of Abbot Hugo of St. Mary's. A man passed Robin's hidden band, driving a fat bullock toward the castle, and following him came an old man with a load of logs for Isambart's fires, and, on the top, sacks of chips and kindling wood.

"That is my man," said Robin, and stepped out and met him.

"Ho, gaffer!" he called. "How much will you take for the load?"

The old man shook his head. "Good master," he answered, "I dare not sell it, for it is for the castle."

"I will give you two gold marks if you lend me your clothes and let me take the load to the castle for you," Robin offered.

The old man's eyes opened wide. "Two gold marks, master? Never in my life have I seen a gold mark, though I once had three silver ones."

"These two are gold," Robin said, showing them. "Now, gaffer, down with you, and lend me your clothes, for there is need for haste."

"Aye," said the old man, "for in a couple of hours or so they will begin to assemble for the hanging of that right good man of Robin Hood's band, and the wood must be unloaded before that."

He got down and, under Robin's direction, stripped off his old rags, which Robin put on. Then, with a stoop in his back and earth rubbed on his face, Robin lifted up his two bundles carefully and laid them on top of the sacks of wood chips, after which he drew on rough leather gloves, such as woodmen use for chopping among thorns to save their hands, and tied the gauntlets of the gloves over his wrists.

"You fear to soil your hands, master?" the old man asked as he gripped his two gold marks—more wealth than he had ever had in his life.

"Aye," said Robin, "for that castle is a dirty place, by all accounts, and I may have to handle more than wood."

"What be in they sacks o' yours, master?" the old man queried, pointing up at the two sacks which Robin had handled so carefully, placing them so that the string with which they were tied would be ready to his hand as he drove the cart.

"A few friends of mine," Robin answered, "who may serve to amuse Isambart and his men."

He whistled, and Little John with half a dozen men stepped out round the old man, who stood, frightened at their sudden appearance.

"They will do you no harm," Robin said kindly, "but will care for you till I am safely inside that nest of thieves. Now, Little John, take good care of him, so that no alarm can be given, and do you and all the rest lie hid till a hulla-baloo begins about the drawbridge and the castle gateway. Then out into the open with you, advance till you are just out of range of their crossbows, and let fly with your arrows at every man who shows a head."

He took from the pocket of the cloak he had laid aside a queer-looking cap of muslin, which he put on his head under the old man's hat. Then he got up on to the cart, took the reins, and drove off toward Evil Hold, while Little John and the others watched him, and muttered prayers for his safety.

How They Got Will Scarlett Back

CHAPTER XIII

~

ithin the castle yard was bustle and excitement, for, in addition to the ordinary tasks of the morning, there was the business of putting up a tall gallows for the hanging of Will Scarlett, and Isambart himself, together with his friend Roger the Cruel, strode about, the two of them in full armour, bestowing an order here and a kick on some unfortunate worker there. Isambart was in high good humour, for nobody but himself had ever been able to lay hands on any man of Robin's band, and he promised himself that he would not rest content with one, but would get together a party of men who knew the ways of Sherwood, and would smoke out the whole band of them. Also he promised himself an hour or so of amusement in torturing Will Scarlett, once the gallows was up and ready, to see if they could wring out of him the secret of Robin's retreat, which nobody seemed able to find, before they hanged him.

The bustle and excitement were at their highest when a tattered old man drove up to the drawbridge, passed the man on sentry duty without being questioned, since both the horse and cart were well known, and passed through the low arch in the great wall that shut in the castle yard and formed the outer defence of the great keep, in which were Isambart's living-rooms, with the dungeons under them. In the entry to the arch, the old man reached back to one of his bundles, jerked the string off the mouth of the sack, and with a push let loose its contents, which went rolling back toward the guard-house, away from the darkness of the arch.

Taking no notice, the old man drove on, straight toward the keep. He was within ten yards of its open portal when Isambart spied him.

"Hey, old fool!" Isambart yelled. "Think you that we store our wood in our banqueting hall? Fetch your cart here!"

Staring at him stupidly, the old man fumbled with the string of his second sack. Isambart took a couple of steps toward the cart, but stopped as a tremendous yelling and screaming came from the direction of the guardhouse. Then the old man got the string off his sack, gave it a push, and out toppled Robin's second beehive at Isambart's feet, just as Robin pulled down the gauze over his face and neck from under his hat, and made a flying leap that landed him almost in the doorway of the keep.

A great cloud of angry bees rose up all over the castle yard, just as the door of the keep slammed in Isambart's face, and he heard the sound of the great bolts being shot home. Then the horse, stung by half a dozen bees at once, shot forward and scattered a group of Isambart's men who were running toward their master, while first Isambart himself, and then Roger the Cruel, yelled and danced as the bees got under their armour and began to sting. They slapped at the hard metal they wore, and only made matters worse, while Isambart's men ran in all directions.

Roger the Cruel, rolling on the ground and squealing as the stings got at him under his armour, spied a dark storehouse built in the outer walls, and made for its shelter, yelling and slapping himself all over, just as a great arrow hummed over the wall and thudded into the earth at Isambart's feet. Isambart, dancing and slapping with his gauntleted hands, stared at it.

"Attacked—attacked by Robin Hood's band!" he shouted. "To me, men, and lower away at the portcullis! Up with the drawbridge!"

But the bees were keeping his men busy, and they crowded round the dark doorway in which Roger the Cruel was trying to shelter himself, with a little cloud of bees buzzing spitefully around the head of every one of them. Isambart's shout went unheard, for they were all shouting at once, and Isambart himself, stopping every now and again to dance and slap himself, made for the chamber in the wall in which was the portcullis gear, to lower it and keep the outlaws out, for now the arrows began to fall thick and fast, and already three of his men were wounded by them before they could get to the shelter of the wall.

Inside the great keep Robin, profiting from his talk with Dickon of Hartshead, darted into a little room to the right of the doorway, where the only man on guard lounged carelessly. In ten seconds the man was lying stunned by a blow from the heavy cudgel Robin carried in addition to his sword, and Robin had the bunch of keys which he saw lying on the table. As the uproar began among the bees outside, Robin swung shut the heavy door which led to the great hall of the keep and the upper apartments, locking it with one of the keys he had taken, and then with another key he unlocked a door at the head of a stairway that led down into the passageway between the dungeons. He locked this door behind him, knowing that he would not return that way.

"Scarlett?" he shouted. "Where are you, good Will?"

"Here I be!" came a weak voice from the end of the corridor.

Robin went along warily, passing a great chamber through the doorway of which shone a red glow from the fire in which the executioner had been heating his implements of torture, and other doors from which unfortunate victims of Isambart's cruelty called out or moaned as he passed. He called again to make sure of the cell in which Scarlett had been placed, found the right key, and flung the door open.

Will Scarlett staggered out, a bloodstained bandage round his head. "I knew you would not fail me, Robin," he said weakly, "but I doubt if I have strength to win back to the greenwood. They have wounded me sorely."

"Courage, good Will," said Robin, "and a breath of fresh air outside this unwholesome place will work wonders. But I think we have time to unlock a few of these doors as we go. We may win some aid from those within, if we could only arm them."

Door after door he unlocked as they went along the corridor to the foot of the stairway, and out crawled a dozen pallid wretches who would have kissed his feet in thankfulness had he let them, while there were four stout fellows who had not been long confined, and one tall man who bowed courteously to Robin and thanked him for his deliverance.

"Who is the hero that hath released me?" he asked.

"Time for that later," said Robin shortly. "Get you a hammer or a pair of great pincers, or anything with which to strike a blow, from their torture chamber, for we may have fighting yet before we win free."

He had now five good men, in addition to those who were so weak from long imprisonment that they were useless, and he set two of them to help Will Scarlett along. Following the instructions Dickon had given him, he found a low-set door in the wall at the foot of the stairs, and, unlocking it, disclosed the black darkness of a slimy passage.

Just then they heard faintly the sound of great thunderous blows above their heads, and Robin smiled grimly at the noise.

"That is Isambart, past doubt," he said. "He is trying to batter in his own front door, by the sound of it."

And so it was, for since Robin had locked the door of the great inner hall, nobody could get at the bolts of the outer door from its inside to open it, and Isambart's only chance was to batter it down, though he knew it would take a good month of carpenters' and smiths' work to make him another like it, to say nothing of the damage to the masonry. Between the locking of the great door on its owner, and the panic wrought by the bees, Robin's men might have advanced and taken the castle that day, if they had only known it. As it was, they hailed in their arrows and wondered why Isambart did not sally out to attack them, not knowing how busy he was inside his own castle yard.

"We must go this way," said Robin, gazing into the darkness of the passage. "One of you fetch me the torch from the far end of the corridor, and I will lead the way."

When the torch was brought he advanced into the passage with it in one hand and his sword in the other, since here was no room to swing his cudgel, in case of attack. But they met with no attack, for this passage was a secret way of Isambart's for carrying out the bodies of his victims. For nearly a quarter of a mile, they judged, they tramped through the dripping, slimy way, until before them daylight showed through the keyhole of an iron door.

"Now let us pray that I have the key of this door," Robin said, and sought among those he had brought. Among them was one that fitted, and he led the way out into a deep arch, beyond which showed the brilliant sunshine of the day, glimmering on water.

They found themselves standing at the top of a steep slope, with the castle wall behind them, and before them the depths of the moat. Beyond in the distance, waiting for them, lay a body of Robin's men, among whom Little John stood up and waved to them to announce that they had been seen, after which he sank down again into the grass.

"We must swim for it," Robin said. "Come on, Will, and let me give you a hand across."

The tall man who had questioned him stepped forward. "Good sir," he said, "do you let me take one side of him, and between us we will bear him up through the water."

"Willingly," said Robin, "but who may you be that talk like a Norman knight, and yet lie in prison at a Norman knight's hands?"

"I am a knight, Sir Richard at Lea," said the other.

"Mercy on us!" Robin exclaimed, startled. "But let us get across this water before we talk about it."

He led the way down the bank, helping Scarlett as he went, and Sir Richard gave the wounded man a lift on his other side. They got across and climbed out, followed by the four men who had had strength to arm themselves, and by two other prisoners. The rest, hopeless and hardly sane after years of Isambart's cruelties, dared not trust themselves to swim the deep moat, and stood by the archway in the wall, staring stupidly.

"Poor wretches," Robin said, looking back at them, "I would that we could have saved them. But if they cannot help themselves, they must wait till we come this way again. Let us march quickly, before we are spied from the castle."

But Sir Isambart and his men were too busy trying to get back into their own castle, and trying to escape the attentions of such of the bees as still buzzed around them, to keep good watch, and Robin with his party were well out of crossbow shot when a great cry from the castle wall told that they had been seen. A little later, a troop of a dozen horsemen clattered out over the draw-bridge, rounded the moat and galloped across the open to cut off the fleeing men. Then from under the rags that disguised him Robin took the silver bugle he had won in the tournament at Nottingham, and blew five blasts on it.

And from the edge of the wood to which Robin and his party advanced there hummed and sang flight after flight of great arrows toward the pursuing horsemen, so that within a minute half their horses were down, and the rest were bolting back toward the shelter of the castle. Robin blew one short blast, and the arrow showers ceased.

"Man," said Sir Richard at Lea, "are you a magician?"

News from the East

CHAPTER XIV

hile Sir Richard wondered, Robin Hood went on toward the forest shades, where, as his men gathered round him and the rescued Will Scarlett, the knight marvelled still more.

"See to our good Will, Little John," Robin bade, "for they have given him a nasty cut over the head, and we must carry him back to our retreat." He turned then to the knight. "And you, sir, though you give me an impossible name, will perhaps come with us for rest and food?"

"Right gladly," the knight answered. "But why do you call the name I gave you impossible?"

"For that Sir Richard at Lea was drowned in the ship that was sunk when he went to join our King Richard fighting in the Holy Land. That is an old tale, and I must be the magician you called me if I am able to rescue a dead man from Isambart's dungeons."

"Isambart's dungeons?" the knight echoed. "But they were the dungeons of Roger whom they call the Cruel. I never saw Isambart de Belame, all the time of my imprisonment."

"This, then, is a mystery," Robin said, puzzled. "Good knight, tell us all your tale as we go back to our camp, and know yourself safe in Sherwood with Robin Hood and his band."

"And who may they be?" the knight asked.

"You mean that you have never heard of Robin Hood?" Little John asked in amazement. "Good knight, where have you been?"

"Jailed from all knowledge these four years past," Sir Richard answered sadly, "so that I know not if my dear daughter be living, nor what hath passed in the outer world."

"Then tell us all the tale," Robin bade, "for so we may help you."

"The tale begins with my wife's dying," the knight said, "at which I determined to go and fight the Saracens with our great king, for so I might forget my grief awhile. Thus I gave my daughter Marian into charge of Abbot Hugo of St. Mary's, and agreed with him that she should be sent to Kirklees. Then, having but little ready money, I borrowed five hundred marks from the Abbot for my gear and the hire of a ship for me and my men, agreeing to pay him fifty marks a year for the use of the money when I should return, and pledging my chief manor as proof that I would pay him. So he holds the deeds of the manor to this day."

"I might have guessed the hand of Abbot Hugo in this dark tale," said Robin. "But tell us the rest."

"Having made all ready, and bidden farewell to my sweet daughter, I took my men to Hull, and there we set sail in a ship bound for Bordeaux, where I had been told I should find others assembling on my errand. But a storm came out of the east when we had been but three hours at sea, and we drove on to the Lincolnshire coast. Whether any other man was saved out of the wreck I do not know, but I was lifted ashore on the end of a broken spar to which I clung, sore wounded with a great cut in the head, and near on senseless. To the men who found me I had strength to bid that they take me to St. Mary's Abbey, and after that I remember no more, for a fever came of the great wound I had got."

"So you do not know if you came to St. Mary's Abbey?" Robin asked.

"I have memory, like a dream, of Abbot Hugo and Roger the Cruel talking together," Sir Richard answered, "and after that a great darkness as the fever came again. I wakened in the dungeons from which you released me, you who call yourself Robin Hood."

"And for how long does the bond hold under which you borrowed the marks from the Abbot?" Robin asked.

"Four years," the knight answered. "Unless it be paid by Michaelmas Day of this year, then my best manor lands are forfeit to Abbot Hugo."

"So," Robin nodded, "all the plot is clear. He would keep you jailed, since even he dare not have you killed, for the full four years, and then the manor would fall to him. Also he would have you think it was Roger the Cruel who held you prisoner, and not Isambart de Belame, for he would have married your daughter Marian to Belame, and so shared up all your possessions between himself and his friend. Now there are yet seven weeks to Michaelmas Day, good Sir Richard."

"And the bond is for seven hundred marks!" said Sir Richard, "while if it were but for seven marks I could not pay it."

"Rest content on that, Sir Richard, and I will lend you the money," Robin said. "It is but a small sum to us."

"Why," said Sir Richard, "only a king could call it a small sum, and who are you that talk so?"

"King in Sherwood, and some small relative to you by marriage," Robin answered with a laugh. "You shall see presently."

those days except at the tables of the nobles. The good friar rolled out a great cask of strong ale, and another cask of wine from a store that they had captured on its way to St. Mary's Abbey, and Little John barely stopped to smack his lips before he set to with a will.

"Hold hard, there, baby," the friar roared at him, "or there will be naught for me to eat by the time I have finished this thimbleful of ale."

"A mighty miracle-worker is our Friar Tuck, Sir Richard," said Little John, "for he is able to make two quarts of good ale go into a thimble."

"That is the third quart," said the friar, "for cooking is a thirsty business."

"Then, good thimble, get you to eating, and leave me to mind my own platter," Little John retorted. "And if you fear lest I should eat too much, cook more next time."

"Nay," said the friar, "for I cook for men, not whales. But I stay not to talk, lest our mighty infant clear the board before I begin."

So he too set to work to satisfy his great appetite, while Sir Richard looked at his daughter's happy face as if he could never take his eyes from her, and Robin told how he had tumbled the beehives off the cart, till they all roared to hear how Sir Isambart had danced about and slapped at his armour when the bees got inside it. They were still very merry when one of the band was seen leading a stranger down the cliff-side path, a big, rough-looking fellow who came up to where Robin sat.

"Master," said the man of the band, "I have brought in this Walter of Ravenscar, for he hath begged a word with you."

"Now welcome, good Walter," Robin greeted the stranger, "for I have heard of you as one of Yorkshire's best archers. Sit and eat with us, and later we will try a bout at the butts with our bows together."

"Right gladly would I, good Robin Hood, but that I come on a sterner errand," Walter answered. "Since we can find none in Yorkshire to help us, my master hath sent me here from Ravenscar to beg aid of you."

"How so?" Robin asked.

"In this way," Walter answered. "Sir Gurth of Ravenscar holds his castle, though he be a Saxon earl, by favour from Red King William to his father, but in the event of trouble not a Norman knight near him will lend him aid, for they hope to see him overthrown and his castle given to one of their own race. And now Ravenscar is in danger."

"And a long way from Sherwood," Robin pointed out.

"Yet there is time," Walter urged. "For the terrible pirate chief whom men call Damon the Monk is ravaging on the coast up by the mouth of Tyne, and my master Sir Gurth hath certain news that in ten days, or more, Damon will sail down to lay waste all the country about us and besiege and take our castle of Ravenscar. So we called on the Normans of Yorkshire for aid, but they laughed and said Damon might hang us, for all they cared."

"They would," Robin commented.

"Then I said to my master that a Saxon rules in Sherwood, and it would be well to seek aid of him. And here I be."

"I must put it to the vote," Robin said, after a moment's reflection, "for all are free men here, and this is outside our own county."

So when their feast was over he assembled the band, and, with Marian and Sir Richard beside him, told them Walter's tale.

"Now what say you, my men?" he asked. "Shall we go against this pirate, and aid the Saxon lord of Ravenscar?"

A veritable forest of hands went up in assent, and a great, deep-throated shout of "Aye!" told that they had only one mind about it.

"There is your answer, Walter," Robin said with a smile. "For you see that if an Englishman do but ask help of an Englishman, he can win it, though how my foresters will fare against a pirate, and such a pirate as this Damon, is more than I can tell."

"We will get him on land, Robin," said Little John, "and maybe treat him to a beehive or two, or so many good arrows that he will think there is a swarm of bees about his ears."

"We must leave you here, Marian," Robin reflected, "and also Will Scarlett will not be well of his wound, and I will leave a score good fellows to guard you while the rest of us are away."

It was all planned out that day, and the next morning Robin and his men set out, to get to the edge of Sherwood and make the rest of their marches by night, under guidance of Walter of Ravenscar. They took with them provisions for five days, after which Sir Gurth of Ravenscar would provide for their needs. Sir Richard at Lea went down to Newark, for he had heard from Robin Hood that there he would find a king's justiciary, with whom he could lay a charge against Abbot Hugo and Sir Isambart for his wrongful imprisonment. But, as it chanced, he was a day too late to find the justiciary, who was on his way northward, and claimed hospitality of Abbot Hugo at St. Mary's, of which more may be said later.

And, of the four men whom Robin rescued from Evil Hold along with Sir Richard, one went back and sought counsel with Sir Isambart de Belame, who was so badly stung by the bees that he could neither sit nor lie down with any comfort. This man was one William, whom Belame had flung into a dungeon for a trifling offence, and now he hoped to win his way back into his master's favour.

"Back again, William!" said Isambart, with vengeful satisfaction. "Well, down you go to the dungeon, then, and I will see that you have a sore back to sleep with. If I had but a hive of bees, they should join you in the dungeon."

"But I bring you great news, Sir Isambart," William said, a little afraid, now, of having trusted himself to his angry master, but still hopeful. "For I can guide you to Robin Hood's most secret retreat."

"Ha!" and Isambart looked eager. "Then we shall lay hands on the villain at last!"

"He is away with his band," William said, "but he hath left Marian, Sir Richard's daughter, in care of a score men, and I thought mayhap you might wish to capture her before you lay in wait for him and his men on their return. I have been with them, and can guide you."

Isambart looked at his man keenly. "If this be true, William," he said, "you shall go to no more dungeons, but if it be a lie, look to yourself, for I will have you skinned alive when I find you have deceived me."

"No deceit, but truth, Sir Isambart," William protested. "Keep me bound beside you till we find out whether I speak truth, and reward me suitably when the prize is yours."

"The prize—yes," Isambart reflected. "With Marian in my hands, I will hold her fortune as well, and though Sir Richard have escaped me we can swear he hath consorted with the outlaw Robin Hood, and so have him outlawed. All will work well for us yet, if only these cursed bee stings would heal. Get to your quarters, William, and I will send for you to guide my men when I have assembled them."

Well pleased with himself, William obeyed, and in Evil Hold the plot was matured while Robin Hood and his men marched toward Ravenscar.

Robin and his men from the greenwood made quick fodder of Damon the Monk and his pirate crew. They thwarted the sacking of Sir Gurth's Castle of Ravenscar cold, burned Damon's ship and captured the prize of his treasures. But their victory celebration was only short lived.

For Will Scarlett came on a big roan horse at a gallop over the ridges toward them and drew rein by Robin Hood's side.

"Robin," he said, "I have ridden night and day to get to you. Isambart de Belame hath burned out our glade, and carried off your wife Marian to Evil Hold, with five of our good men whom he captured."

The Black Knight Appears

CHAPTER XV

wo and twenty horses were all that Sir Gurth could find or borrow, and these he lent gladly enough to Robin and his men, who armed themselves to the teeth from the plunder of Damon's long dragon-boat before they set out for Evil Hold, Robin and Little John at the head of the mounted men, and Friar Tuck with Will Scarlett and Much following on with those for whom horses could not be found. For the first time since he had taken to the greenwood Robin's face was set and stern, for he could hold his own against any man with a jest on his lips and a smile in his eyes, but this carrying off of Marian was a different thing.

"From this Isambart I saved her," he said, "knowing that she looked on the man with fear, as would any maid who would avoid evil. Now, whether Isambart have harmed one hair of her head or no, by this act against me he has brought doom to Evil Hold."

"Friend," said Sir Gurth, "it is no small thing to attack a strong castle, such as this you call Evil Hold."

"Attack?" said Robin grimly. "Not only will I attack, but I will send Evil Hold flaming to the sky and make an end of it. So shall honest men breathe more freely, and their wives no longer shiver and tremble at the name of Isambart de Belame. He hath done wrongs enough."

He set out to ride fast and far. By night marches only had the outlaws come to Ravenscar, to the taking of the long dragon-boat, but they rode back, and those under Friar Tuck marched back, both by day and night, hurrying ever, as they thought of Marian and the five good fellows whom Isambart had taken off to his hold. Dusk of the third day was falling when Robin and his party dismounted on the edge of the woods, and looked out on Evil Hold.

"Look, good Robin," said Little John, with a sob in his voice, and pointed toward the great castle on its height. "In one way we are too late to aid, for we shall speak with those five no more."

Above the outer wall of the castle reared a skeleton framework, and on it swung five black figures, still and ominous. A long time Robin looked at his dead men in silence, and then he raised his bow and put the grasp of its arch against his lips.

"By our Lady the Virgin," he said slowly, "I will not rest from war against this evil man until he is lifeless as are they."

"Do we wait for the good friar and the others?" Little John asked. "For that castle is in truth a stronghold, and Isambart hath men a-plenty to guard it. We have no small task before us, master Robin."

"We rest this night," Robin answered, "but by dawn we must be astir against them. He will not have dared to harm Marian, for he wants her lands, as Abbot Hugo wanted Sir Richard's manor. By dawn I will have a plan formed to make an end of this Isambart."

"But who comes here?" Little John asked. "What if it prove to be Isambart himself?"

"Too tall for Isambart," said Robin, "nor did Isambart ever sit a horse like this man. He carries a blank shield, see."

From the direction of the castle a strange knight came toward them, riding a great black horse, and armed all in black, with visor down. It was strange that he neither reined in nor showed any sign of alarm at sight of more than a score of armed men on the track, for in those troubled times such a lone rider might expect attack. But he came on like a tower of black iron, and they saw a great battle axe hanging by his saddle bow.

"A bold man," said Robin, admiringly. "Knight," he called, "what do you ride at on these forest ways?"

The Black Knight reined in, and when he spoke his voice sounded hollow from between the bars of his visor.

"I do as I will, to whom I will," he answered, "but for this present I seek shelter for my horse and myself in the forest."

"Yet there is a strong castle behind you that would give shelter," Robin pointed out, "if you are on Count John's affairs."

"Count John's affairs are very near my own," said the knight.

"Then in that castle is a man of his, and we will have pleasure in killing you with him when we set about the castle," Robin said. "Get you gone, for we, being more than a score, would not set about one man."

"There is a mystery here," the knight said thoughtfully, "for you are not armed as Normans arm, nor as the Saxons. And why do you propose to attack yonder castle?"

"For many reasons," Robin answered, which you, being John's man, may not hear. Get gone, to the castle or elsewhere."

"Though John's affairs are very near mine, I am not John's man," the knight answered, "and if there be cause for the pulling down of that castle I might help, at a pinch. But is there cause?"

"Right good cause," Robin answered. "If you should care to eat with us, I can tell you some of the cause, good knight, and you may see whether it is worthwhile to swing that great axe of yours beside us—or against us, if it please you. For if you are for that castle's owner, it will give me great pleasure to kill you."

The Black Knight dismounted from his horse, a great, strong figure of a man. "I will eat with you," he said, "and we may discuss this matter while we eat. To my thought, these strong castles are too plentiful about the country, but whether this one should be attacked or no is a matter for grave thought. You shall state your reasons."

So, when they had all tended their horses, and settled round a fire deeply set in the forest shade, so that Isambart's sentries could not see the flame, Robin told the tale of how Sir Richard at Lea had been imprisoned in Evil Hold for nearly four years, so that Abbot Hugo might have his manor and Isambart might have his daughter and the rest of his lands. The Black Knight, who had raised his visor to eat, but kept his helmet on so that they could see little of his face, listened to the story.

"Right well I know that Sir Richard," he said, "for I was present when he was knighted by King Henry. But where do you who tell this tale come into it? What have Sir Richard's woes to do with you?"

"Sir Richard's daughter is my wife," Robin answered.

"Yet even then, since you have the maid as your wife, and this Sir Isambart have not harmed you, it is not your quarrel," said the knight.

Robin pointed through the trees in the direction of the castle. "She lies prisoner in that hold, captured in my absence, when this Sir Isambart burned my home and took my men to hang them from his castle wall," he said. "Knight, by your talk you are Norman, but so is my wife's father, for there are some good Normans, and I would that the best of them all, our King Richard, were back to right some of these wrongs in England. If you choose to help us, then we are glad of you, but if you would leave us, go free, for you have eaten of our bread and meat."

"Of a surety I will help you," the Black Knight promised, "for of this burning of homes and carrying off of women—aye, and hanging of men too!—there is too much, and it is time these robber barons were taught their lesson. But how will you, with not more than a score men, go up against such a castle as that?"

"Aye, how, good Robin?" asked Little John. "Shall we sit under the wall and scratch a hole in it with our fingernails?"

"What name was that he called you?" the knight asked quickly.

"My own name—Robin Hood. But remember, good knight, you have promised us your aid!"

The knight laughed softly to himself, and for a few moments sat in thought. "Aye, I have promised," he said at last. "Yet, Robin Hood, will you scratch a hole in the wall of the castle and crawl through, as your man here asked just now? For it is no small thing to attack such a place."

"I have thirty more men to come," Robin said shortly, "and when it is time I will scratch you such a hole in the wall of this castle as shall leave it toppling, if a dozen of the best of you come with me."

"You have a plan then?" the knight asked.

"I have more, a key by which to enter the very keep itself. For when I had rescued Sir Richard along with my own man from their dungeons, I kept the key of the postern at back of the castle, and now wait only for the rest of my men to come up before attacking from the inside, and opening the gate to the main party of my men."

"So you rescued Sir Richard yourself?" the Black Knight asked curiously. "But how did you get that key?"

Robin told of his stratagem of the beehives, and the knight sat and thought over it for a long time.

"A bold game to play, outlaw," he said, "but ever the bold game wins. When your men come up, I will either come with you by the postern, or lead the main attack for you, as you will."

Robin looked at the knight's mighty frame. "Then lead me the main attack," he said, "for craft will mainly serve inside, but such strength as yours will be needed in the attack on the gate." "Where then are these thirty men of yours?" the knight asked. "They are yet to come from our attack on the pirate, Damon the Monk, by Ravenscar," Robin answered frankly.

The knight's eyes gleamed from the depths of his helmet. "Now say," he said, "do you tell me that you dared go against that great pirate?"

"We killed him and burnt his ship," Robin answered carelessly, and yawned. "And, having ridden far this day, knight, it is time we slept, for there is hard work before us to-morrow."

"So you, an outlaw, have rid our coasts of that evil thief?" the knight remarked thoughtfully.

"Knight," said Robin, with a trace of harshness, "I have no liking for the way you harp on my outlawry, and I tell you that, with the laws as they are, I had as soon be out of the law as within it, since such as this Isambart de Belame are not outlawed, but do their evil deeds and no man checks them."

The knight made no answer, but sat looking into the embers of their fire, as if deep in thought. Then he stood up.

"I will go and sleep by my horse," he said, "but you have given me much on which to think, Robin Hood. Some day, perhaps, you may know my name, but before that I will help you in this business of the castle over on the hill there, for that is a foul tyrant who hath no place either within the law or out of it."

He went off, leaving Robin sitting by the dying fire, wondering how Marian fared in her imprisonment in Evil Hold, and longing for Friar Tuck to come with his men, so that they could attack.

And, thinking of her whom he loved and had married in the greenwood, he forgot to think who this black-armoured knight, beyond question a Norman noble, could be, or why he should choose to give his aid to the outlaws of Sherwood.

The End of Evil Hold

CHAPTER XVI

 reaths of autumn mist shrouded the forest ways next day when Friar Tuck tramped in with the rest of Robin Hood's men—except for the wounded left at Ravenscar—and asked what plans Robin had made for the attack on Evil Hold. The Black Knight—for they knew him by no other name— stood by and listened while Robin told his men how Isambart had hanged the five he had captured, and many a promise of vengeance was made as they heard.

"Now, for the sake of Marian, we must lose no time," Robin said. "This knight hath promised me that he will lead the attack on the main gateway of the castle, while I, who know of a way in, will take a score of you who can swim, and attack from the inside while Isambart and his men are busy defending the drawbridge."

"But," said the knight, at whom all looked as he stood among them with his visor down, "there must be some signal, so that neither your men nor those I lead attack too soon, for else this Isambart will dispose of one party first and then turn on the other."

"So be it then," Robin answered, "let us trust the eye of our Will Scarlett and the strength of his arm and bow. Will's arrow will fly over the Evil Hold to signal us both. I will then with these men swim the moat at the back of the castle, and when you see us up against the wall itself, then do you attack in front. They will muster to resist you, and leave me to do what I will in the keep. And I want Dickon of Hartshead, who helped in the building of the place, to come with me and show me the ways of it, since Marian is prisoned there."

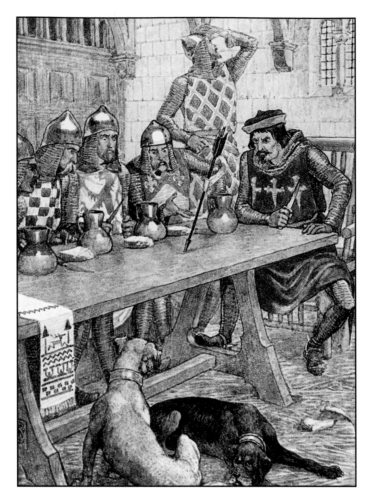

Whang! To Isambart and his men something had seemed to snap through the air from above their heads, and lo! here, sticking in the table before Sir Isambart, was Will Scarlett's signal arrow.

Only for a moment did de Belame lose his presence of mind. He looked up to the walls of the castle and shouted: "'Twas shot from a hole in the sky! What means this?"

And his face went fierce and dark with fury, as he shouted even louder: "Look all, there are strange powers against us! Up now and search for them!"

But already Robin had taken Little John, and Dickon, and eighteen more, armed only with swords, since he reckoned on getting at Isambart's armoury once they were inside, and knew that if they took bows the strings would only get wet and become useless in crossing the moat. They could not have had a better day, for mists lay over all the countryside, and, moving as only foresters can, they were able to make their way to the very edge of the moat unseen. As it was, they came up toward the back of the castle, where little or no watch was kept, and there waited awhile, for the mists were deepening to fog, and Robin hoped, if it thickened a little more, to swim the moat unseen by the men who walked the walls.

Unseen he crossed, a little after noon, and helped man after man up the inner bank until all were across. Then they crawled warily up the steep slope and gained the shelter of the archway which hid the iron door leading into Isambart's secret passage, and then the chain of watchers whom the knight and Friar Tuck had posted passed back word that it was time to begin the main attack, at which the larger party of the outlaws, led by the Black Knight, moved out from the forest toward the main gate.

The key to the iron door squealed in its rusty lock as Robin turned it, and as he thrust the door open he heard a shout from the battlements, at which he feared that he had been seen in the archway. But it was the cry passed on from Isambart that the main gate was about to be attacked, and after it a trumpet blew for the assembly of the castle garrison. One by one Robin and his men filed into the secret way, and in single file marched down it, in pitch darkness, for after their crossing of the moat they had no means of making a light.

Cut off from all hearing of what was passing above them, they reached the door that gave on to the corridor of dungeons and Isambart's torture chamber, and here Robin, who had kept only the one key, called forward Little John to come up beside him.

"'Tis but a flimsy door of wood, John," he whispered, "and I have no key to it. But it opens outward, and your great shoulder may serve with my help to make us a way."

He put his own shoulder against the door, and felt it give slightly. For a moment they listened, but there was no sound in the corridor beyond, and then Little John put his mighty bulk against the door with Robin. At a tremendous heave by them both the woodwork about the lock splintered and gave way, and they half fell into the dim light of the dungeon corridor. A moaning came from one of the cells, but no other sound.

"Dickon," Robin bade, "before our work here is finished, do you get the keys of these cells and let loose any poor wretches you find within. But now we have another door to force at the top of these stairs, before we win out to the entrance of the keep itself."

He went forward into the torture chamber, which was unlighted now, and there found two great hammers used for riveting fetters on Isambart's prisoners. One he took for himself, and the other for Little John, and the two of them led the way up the stair.

"Stand back, Robin," Little John bade, "and give me that heavier hammer, for there is room for but one to swing a blow, here."

He felt about the door till he had found its lock, while one of the band passed up the torch which burned at the far end of the dungeon corridor. Little

John spat on his hands, took a grip of the great hammer, and whirled it above his head, bringing it down with a crash on the lock of the door. They saw a crack of light show beyond, and gripped their swords as the hammer swung again, and with a second crashing blow burst them a way out to the entrance of the keep.

Four men, whom Isambart had left to guard his prisoners when he went to the defence of the drawbridge, started forward, but Little John's hammer took one in the chest and sent him flying against another, so that two were down with the one blow. Robin accounted for a third, and the fourth bolted with a yell for Isambart's great hall, but never reached it, for the whole score of Robin's men were close behind him, hot and eager. They surged into the hall, and paused, for at the far side, bound in a chair, sat Marian all alone, with a great parchment spread on the table before her, and an inkhorn and quill beside it.

"Robin!" she cried. "Robin—he would have made me sign away my lands to him, but I would not."

"Time for that afterward, dear wife," Robin answered, stooping to kiss her as he drew his sword to cut her bonds. "Now, any two of you but Dickon or Little John, take her out by the secret passage, and across the moat to safety. Here is no place for women, if we would win the castle."

He stayed but for a word more with her, then, as two volunteered to escort her out to the safety of the forest, followed Dickon of Hartshead to Isambart's armoury. A dozen of his men went out to the shattered door of the keep, which Isambart himself had had to batter down after Robin had locked him out of his own castle, and which had not yet been repaired. While Robin and Dickon were busy getting bows these dozen had to stand the attack of Roger the Cruel and half a score of men-at-arms who had seen that all was not well inside the castle. Little John crashed Roger to earth as a great arrow sang by his ear and pinned another man so that he fell, and Robin shouted joyfully.

"Bows, men—bows for all! Stand aside and let us at them!"

The dozen fell back against the walls, and a hail of arrows finished off the men Roger had fetched. Now they could hear the roaring attack that went on by the drawbridge, led by the Black Knight, and Robin served out a bow and full quiver from Isambart's armoury to each man.

"Out and at them," he bade, "while they meet the attack from outside."

The Black Knight had led his party on with a rush, and they came at the drawbridge out of the mist while

Little John was battering a way through the door at the top of the dungeon stair; Friar Tuck, puffing as he ran, bore the biggest ladder he could find, to help in crossing the moat if they were too late to win the drawbridge, and two others also carried ladders they had taken from a farm nearby. The Black Knight, leading the whole of them in spite of his armour, was still a score yards from the end of the drawbridge when the alarm sounded within the castle wall and the end of the bridge swung into the air, for their advance had been seen by the sentry on the wall.

"Into the moat with the ladders!" the Black Knight commanded. "They will save us from sinking in our armour." For Robin's men were heavily armed, while the knight himself was in complete mail from head to foot. And never had they seen a man so active; he was like a cat on his feet, in spite of the weight of metal he carried.

Splash went the ladders at his word, and he leaped into the water, grasping one and pushing it across as he swam. Crossbow bolts rattled on him, but they were no more than flies buzzing, for all the notice he took of them. Friar Tuck, who plunged in beside him, grabbed the end of the ladder just in time as the water closed over his head, and came up blowing like a whale.

"I had sooner drink wine," he remarked. "This moat hath an unpleasant flavour, like its owner."

The other ladders pitched in, and by the aid of all three a dozen men got safely across while the rest of the band made the crossbowmen keep away from the slits in the wall, for arrows hailed through with deadly accuracy, and though Isambart cursed and raved at his men he could not get them to face the shafts from the long bows. The Black Knight and Friar Tuck hauled up their ladder and stood under the shelter of the wall, and Isambart, spying them, yelled to his men to tumble stones down on them. But as surely as a man tried to roll a stone over, an arrow found him, for the party on the other side of the moat had eyes keen enough to pierce the mist.

They could not have chosen a better time, had they known it, for Isambart had lost heavily in his attack on the forest stronghold when he carried off Marian, and he had twenty men out on a raiding party as well, while Robin and his men inside had already accounted for Roger the Cruel and more than a dozen of the garrison. There were not sixty men in all to aid Isambart in holding the gate, though the proper strength of the castle was rated at not less than a hundred, and of these sixty a dozen were already dead or wounded by the arrows that flew with such deadly accuracy from Robin's men.

Inside, Robin could see across the yard the open recess in the wall, above the entrance arch, in which was the gear for raising and lowering the drawbridge and portcullis. He could see, too, how Isambart tried to get his men up for the defence and knew that all was not well with them.

"Now," he said, "if some dozen of you here keep us a clear way to the drawbridge gear with your bows, the rest of us may charge across and lower the bridge for our fellows outside, and mayhap get the portcullis up as well. To me, Little John, and four more—the rest of you to your bows, and spare not the arrows."

They went at it with a run, and were almost at the gatehouse before Isambart spied them. He roared to his men to guard the stair, but the humming arrows made it a place of death, and Robin and Little John, who still carried his great hammer, were at the top before a man could come at them. By the time Isambart's men thought to counter the attack with crossbows, Robin's party were safe in the open recess, and still the flying arrows kept back those who would attack. Isambart himself tried it, but so many arrows rattled on his mail that he was literally driven back by their weight, and could not come at the recess, for all the defences of the castle were constructed to stand attack from outside, not from within, and against men shooting from the door of their own keep the defenders were helpless.

Now with a dozen great blows of his hammer Little John smashed the ratchet that held up the bridge, and it crashed down with such force that it broke in half, yet left enough for Robin's men outside to cross by it, wet-footed. Then Little John and Robin each took one of the windlasses of the portcullis, and slowly it began to rise as the outlaws poured across the broken bridge.

First through the rising portcullis was Friar Tuck, his robe tucked up in his girdle, and a sword in his hand—but there was nobody to strike, for all Isambart's men that were left on their feet fled toward the keep. Isambart himself, mailed and with his visor down, stood his ground, and Friar Tuck would have made at him, but the Black Knight held him back.

"My baron—my quarrel," he said, words which the friar could not then understand. But the knight's hand on his shoulder wrenched him back as Robin came running down from the windlass recess, eager to engage with the man who had carried off his wife.

"Back!" the Black Knight ordered, in a tone there was no disputing. "This man is mine—I will engage him."

At the order all men stood still to watch, except those who fought with Isambart's followers in the entrance of the keep. They saw how the Black Knight came up to Isambart, apparently careless, with his battle axe swinging lightly in his hand, though it was of a weight that few men would have cared to swing. When Isambart thrust at him with his long sword he was not in the way

of the thrust, for he moved like lightning, yet always with apparent carelessness. Three times Isambart thrust, and three times the thrust went wide, before the battle axe flashed and fell once only, and Isambart crashed to earth to move no more.

Then a cry from the gateway of the keep warned Robin that his men there were hard beset, and he ran to their aid. By the time that business was finished, there was no more resistance left, but Evil Hold was at the mercy of him and his men. And now, at a thought, he swung round suddenly, looking out into the castle yard.

"The Black Knight—where is he?" he shouted.

"Legging it, Robin," Friar Tuck answered. "For he went out through the arch and over the bridge, and by this time, if he keep the pace at which he started, he hath reached his horse and gone, without a word of farewell to any of us."

"We might have known it," Robin said regretfully. "If any man of you see that knight again, on your knees to him and beg mercy of him. Only one man in the world swings a battle axe in such fashion, and only one man is so like a cat on his feet. That was our King Richard, and we were all blind not to know him."

"King or cat, there he goes," Little John said, and pointed.

And, through the opening under the raised portcullis, they could see the Black Knight's horse trotting away. Robin shook his head regretfully.

"Still, he helped us, and had he not approved us he would not have done that," he said. "Now I know why he kept his helmet and refused to tell his name. They say he has left not a castle standing in Lincolnshire, and he used his strength to help us make an end of this Evil Hold."

"It still stands," Little John reminded him.

"But not for long," Robin said, "for as we have made an end of the master, so will we make an end of his hold, lest some other evil baron come to oppress the people round from its shelter."

He bade them take barrels of pitch, of which there was plenty, and place one in each room of the great keep, together with all the firewood they could find. When all women in hiding had been sought out and sent from the castle, and the prisoners had been released, they fired the place, and from every window and arrow slit the black smoke streamed out on the misty air, to be presently shot with tongues of flame. They shattered the windlasses of the portcullis, so that it could be raised no more, and the drawbridge was already a broken thing. A party of them dug at the outer bank of the moat where it was lowest, and all the water went flowing out across the plain, so that there was no outer defence left for the wall, and in later days men came and took away the stones for building their homes, since Robin and his men left them unharmed.

But the great keep flamed up, a pillar of fire visible for miles round, and the poor people whom Isambart had oppressed and taxed came and blessed Robin Hood and his men for the work they had done in freeing them from a wicked tyrant. Far into the night the castle blazed like a great torch, and in the end went crashing down to a mere heap of cracked stones, over which brambles grew in later days, and foxes made their dens among them.

But Roger the Cruel, recovering in time from the great blow that had laid him low, crept away while the Black Knight and Isambart fought each other, and made his way down the dungeon stair, out by the secret passage, and across the moat. Thus he escaped his just doom, and out of that came bitter trouble on a later day.

The Game of Buffets

CHAPTER XVII

~

ithin a week of their return from the burning of Evil Hold, Robin Hood and his men feasted, right merrily, with Marian to grace their table. They had repaired the damage wrought by Isambart in their secret glade, for the baron's men had overlooked the two caves in which most of the outlaws' stores were kept, and had done little beyond burning the huts in the glade, since they were in a hurry to carry off Marian before Robin and the greater part of his men could fall on them. The men wounded in the fight with the pirate in what is now called Robin Hood's Bay were beginning to come back from Ravenscar, and all were eager to prepare for a winter of comfort in the forest depths when Robin heard that Abbot Hugo of St. Mary's intended to visit his brother at Nottingham.

News had reached the Sherwood Forest that Sir Richard returned to the Abbey to reclaim his land, bringing with him an unidentified palmer. There he found the Abbot with the King's Justiciary. Abbot Hugo was outraged when Sir Richard laid down two bags filled with the seven hundred gold marks to pay his bond. But the true surprise came when the palmer revealed himself as King Richard, who promised to bring the Abbot to trial for the unjust imprisonment of Sir Richard.

"Since his place as Abbot is in danger he will surely take at least a part of his hoard with him and he will try to lay up a store against the tie when King Richard comes back to right Abbot Hugo's wrong against Sir Richard," Robin

commented. "I would that I had been in the hall to see our King beard the Abbot and tell him the truth about himself."

On a clear autumn day, when the brown leaves fluttered down in the forest, Hugo went his way toward Nottingham with three friars in attendance, and Guy of Gisbourne with all the men-at-arms the Abbey could furnish to guard them. Guy with ten men led the way, and then came the Abbot riding, with six men leading heavily laden baggage mules and the three friars on foot, and behind these, as rearguard, were another ten men-at-arms. A merchant begged the protection of their escort, and the Abbot graciously allowed him to join the party as they entered the forest itself.

They had just crossed an open glen when Robin's men fell on them, so suddenly that the whole struggle was over almost as soon as it began. Guy of Gisbourne said that his horse bolted with him, but whether his spurs helped it was never known, though he and his ten men were outnumbered three to one, while the rearguard, seeing men swarming between them and the Abbot in front, took to their heels without a blow, so great was their fear of the outlaws. So there were left the Abbot with his friars and the mules, and the merchant, who, having no goods with him, seemed very little disturbed, but pulled his hood down over his face and waited on events.

"Greeting, Hugo," said Robin Hood. "Get down from that tall horse, and let us have a word together."

Trembling with helpless rage, the Abbot dismounted, and stood with his three monks, while Robin's men took away those who had led the mules, and investigated the contents of the packs.

"But a week ago, on Michaelmas Day," said Robin, "I lent seven hundred good gold marks to St. Mary's Abbey. It looks as if you have had the goodness to repay it already, by the packs on these mules."

"Robbery and outrage!" the Abbot breathed fiercely.

"Aye," Robin said, "Robbery and outrage. Harkye, Abbot, 'tis but a fortnight since that I rescued Marian, daughter of Sir Richard at Lea, from the clutch of Isambart of Evil Hold, and she sat before a parchment that Isambart would have had her sign, giving all her lands and goods to him."

"I know nothing of this, outlaw," the Abbot cried.

"Nothing?" Robin mocked him. "What if I tell you that no man of all Isambart's men, nor Isambart himself, could draw up such a parchment? And what if I tell you further that the parchment was drawn up by your clerk, in St. Mary's Abbey, by your order?"

"It is false!" the Abbot shouted.

"Good Friar Tuck," Robin said, "bring that clerk here."

Friar Tuck waddled out from among the trees, and the merchant turned to look at him. He led by the ear a lean-looking, miserable monk, who appeared as badly scared as ever he had been in his life.

"Now, Abbot Hugo," Robin said, "you will surely know your own clerk. Know, too, that he hath a taste for fishing, and when he went fishing this morning my men took him, for I needed a witness to this meeting of ours. Say now, shall he tell his tale?"

Hugo shook his head. "Let him keep silence, and I will confess that I ordered the parchment to be written for Isambart," he said sulkily. For he considered that, if once his clerk began to talk, there was no telling how many other evil deeds he might confess.

Robin nodded his satisfaction. "Now, Lord Abbot," he said, "there is the matter of seven hundred marks lent to St. Mary's by me, Robin Hood—"

"I know nothing of that," Hugo interrupted.

"Patience—you will in good time, for the score against you is a long one," Robin answered. "After that matter, there is the imprisonment of Sir Richard at Lea in Evil Hold, for which payment must be made."

"I had no hand in that!" Hugo cried.

"Friar Tuck, prod that clerk and make him talk," Robin ordered, "for he was witness when Isambart and Roger the Cruel—"

"Nay," the Abbot yelled, "Let him keep quiet, and I will confess that too. I shared the guilt of Sir Richard's imprisonment with Isambart."

The merchant, leaning against a tree with two men keeping guard over him, sighed and nodded to himself.

"We will say for that another seven hundred marks, Abbot," Robin suggested, "and so you get off cheaply."

"I am a ruined man!" the Abbot moaned.

"There is also the matter of certain good men I lost when I went to rescue Sir Richard's daughter Marian and burn Evil Hold," Robin pursued calmly. "It is, I know, the custom of such as you to leave the wives and children of such men to starve if the men are killed, but I have another mind about it. A hundred gold marks, to divide among the widows and fatherless children, Abbot, is a small price to pay."

"Robbery and outrage!" the Abbot wailed again.

"The custom of fat abbots is ever robbery and outrage," Robin retorted sternly, "but their sins come back on them at times. Little John, let us look at what the mules carry."

Robin's men, directed by Little John, had been busy stripping the packs off the mules and laying out their contents, which were mainly bags of gold and silver coin, a service of massive silver plate, a bundle of parchment deeds, and some bales of robes and rich cloth which the Abbot had thought he would take to Nottingham to entrust to his brother's care.

"Good store for a ruined man," Robin commented. "Set us aside fifteen hundred marks in payment of the Abbot's just debts, and choose us out the best bale of stuffs for the queen of Sherwood to clothe herself for the winter, Little John, and his holiness shall dance for the rest."

While they counted the money, and the merchant watched them silently, Robin turned to the Abbot again.

"Now, Hugo, our Friar Tuck shall carol us a lively song, and you shall edify us by dancing to it on the turf. Strike up, friar, and let us see the holy man trip a measure."

"But I have rheumatism!" the Abbot protested. "I cannot dance—I am no dancer. Oh, my wealth, my sins! This is outrage against Holy Church! It is impossible."

"Take an arrow apiece and prick him in the calf, Much and Scarlett," Robin bade, as Friar Tuck began to bellow out a melody. "We will give him a cure for his rheumatism."

At the first touch of the arrow point through his robe the Abbot leaped in the air with a squeal, and presently he had gathered up his robe to clear his fat legs, and was hopping and skipping like a mad rabbit. By the time Friar Tuck left off singing, the Abbot was panting for want of breath, and most of Robin's men were helpless with laughter.

"A right good measure, Abbot," Robin said gravely, "and a sure cure for the rheumatism. Now take your clerk, and your monks and mules, and get on your way, but write no more parchments for thieving barons, nor imprison good knights, or it will go far worse when I catch you again. If it were not that our good King Richard will bring you to trial in his own time, and I trust hang you for your oppressions, I had not let you go now, but I leave you to the justice that is within the law."

While the outlaw band watched the Abbot's men repack his goods on the mules—Robin had one last lesson for the Abbot.

Thus Hugo rode off facing backwards, his feet lashed tight under his mule. Robin's merry men laughed even more loudly as the Abbot's sorry and crestfallen gathering set off on their way.

Little John called out to his chief.

"Ho, Robin, here is a tall, hooded merchant still wanting our attention. Do we let him follow the Abbot down to Nottingham?"

"Not so," said Robin. "How much money hath he?"

"Forty marks," Little John answered, "if the count tally with his statement when we asked him."

"Search him and see," Robin bade.

So they took off the bag at his waist to count its contents.

"He tells truth," Little John reported, while the merchant stood composed, with folded arms, "but he refuses to remove his cowl."

"That is his own affair," Robin said. "Being a truthful man we will fine him twenty marks for being in the company of a lying thief like Abbot Hugo, and let him go."

"Now by the Rood, this is too much!" the merchant said, and, as Little John tossed the bag back at him after taking from it twenty gold marks, he took two quick steps forward, and dealt the giant a flat-handed blow at which he staggered and fell. A roar went up from the outlaws, and two men drew their swords as Little John got to his feet.

"Hold!" Robin Hood cried with a laugh. "He had the right of it. John, where were your manners, that you did not hand back the bag, for this is a man of substance, and no mere churl? Pick up the bag and give it to him as to a man worth respect."

"He hath a good muscle," Friar Tuck said, with a chuckle. "Merchant, will you try a game of buffets with me?"

"Willingly, if I knew the game," the merchant answered.

"A simple game," the friar assured him, coming forward. "See, now, you stand there, and I stand here. I give you such a buffet as you gave our infant John, who is too small and weak to stand such games, and if you can get on your feet again, you may give me one back." For Friar Tuck reckoned on avenging the mighty blow his friend had suffered.

"Strike, then," said the merchant, "for I will play your game."

Friar Tuck rolled back his sleeve and gave the tall merchant such a blow as had sent many a man rolling, but it did not produce even a quiver of the merchant's frame.

"Saint Peter, but this is an iron merchant!" said the Friar. "Now smite, unless you be pegged to the ground."

The merchant gave him a careless wallop, and over he went like a ninepin. He got on his feet again in a dazed way.

"Enough, good merchant," he said, "for the Church is overthrown. But by the ringing in my head the bells are sound enough."

"My turn," Robin Hood said, a little nettled at seeing his two strongest men felled so easily.

Just then he saw through the trees a pair riding toward them. They were Marian, his wife, and her father, Sir Richard at Lea.

Robin turned back to the merchant and said:

"Stand for it, merchant, while I give you a buffet, and then I will take one from you."

He put all his strength into his blow, and the merchant rocked on his feet a little and shook his head, as if the blow had been no light one. But, to Robin's surprise, he did not fall, though no one man of the band could keep on his feet after one of Robin's buffets.

"My turn," said the merchant, and Robin braced himself for the blow.

The merchant smiled, bared his arm, and gave so stout a blow full on Robin's breast that the outlaw was hurled some feet away and almost fell to the ground. He kept his feet, however, and coming to the merchant from whose face the cowl had dropped away by reason of the violence of his blow, he said:

"By the sweet Virgin, but there is pith in thy arm, merchant—if merchant thou art—a stalwart man thou."

There is pith in your arm said ROBIN HOOD

At this very moment Sir Richard at Lea leaped from his saddle, and doffing his hat ran forward, crying, "'Tis the King! Kneel, Robin!" The knight knelt on his knees before the King, who now thrust the cowl from off his head of brown hair, and revealed the handsome face and blue eyes, in which a proud but genial light shone, of Richard Coeur-de-Lion. Then he tore aside the black robes he wore, showing beneath the rich silk surtout blazoned with the leopards of Anjou and the fleur-de-lys of France.

Robin and his outlaws kneeled at the sight.

"By the soul of my father," said Richard with a gay laugh, "but this is a right fair adventure. Why do ye kneel, good Robin? Art thou not king of the greenwood?"

"My lord, the King of England," said Robin, "I love thee and fear thee, and would crave thy mercy for myself and my men for all the deeds which we have done against thy laws. Of thy goodness and grace give us mercy!"

"Rise, Robin, for by the Trinity, I have never met in the greenwood a man so much after my heart as thou art," said the King. He caught Robin by the hand and lifted him to his feet.

"But," said King Richard, "what of the stolen deer? What of the prelates of the Church robbed, and the spoiling of my barons who passed this way? Why should I pardon you?"

"Lord King," he said, "if I have spoiled such as Abbot Hugo, I have but taken the spoils of a thief. If I have robbed a baron, I have done no more harm than when I plundered the long dragon-boat of Damon the Monk, pirate and murderer. I have wronged no woman and harmed no man who lives justly."

"And will you be judge as to who lives justly?" King Richard asked.

"I will be judge of what I know," Robin answered hardily, looking his King in the face, "and deal justly when I have judged. I have spoiled a thieving Prior to send money to your ransom, that we might have a king worth serving in England. I have made oppressors afraid of their evil deeds, and lived cleanly in the greenwood while barons did foul things in castles. You, sire, know what manner of place was Evil Hold, that a certain black knight helped my men to assault."

"True—true enough," Richard answered moodily. "But what of the deer? There you have broken the laws."

"I confess our fault," Robin asked frankly, "yet, outlawed as we were, how else could we live? Sire, these men have fought with you, and not one of them but has prayed for your return to this misruled land. Grant them pardon, and do as you will with me."

"Nay, Robin," the King answered with a smile, "all or none. Now this I will do for you. All that has been shall be forgotten, and you shall be restored every man to his rights, while I will make you warden of Sherwood, with such men as you may choose to serve under you, and with such pay as is fitting to the place. So let it be," rejoiced the King, "and is this fair lady she who hath left honours and lands for love of thee?"

Fair Marian cast herself upon her knees before the King, who gave her his hand to kiss, after which he raised her to her feet.

"Come," said the King, "thou hast given up much to come to thy good archer, fair lady. I can only agree that thou hast chosen a bold man and a brave one. Thou wert ward of mine, and I give thee willingly where thou hast already given thyself."

So saying the King joined the hands of Robin and Marian, both of whom felt very happy in having the King himself pardon them for so willfully acting against his rights.

"Now, all," said Robin, "cheer your good King, for never has this England known such a king and fighter as our King Richard."

They responded with cheers that rang till the forest echoed, and Abbot Hugo, riding down toward Nottingham, forgot to curse over the loss of his gold while he spurred on at such a pace that his followers could hardly keep up with him. Friar Tuck led forward the supposed merchant's horse for him to mount.

"Lord King," he said, "I would that you had time to dine with us, now we are no longer outlaws, for then you might let fall some word that would teach me the secret of the blow that felled me."

"Let us at the least give you escort to Nottingham," Robin urged.

But King Richard shook his head. "I travel alone and fast, on my way to France," he answered. "See that you brave men do loyally and touch the deer no more, for this night a free pardon for you all will lie in the hands of Robert de Rainault in Nottingham, and your inlawing shall be cried in every town in the county. So fare you well, Warden of Sherwood, and see that you do your duty till I come again."

And with a wave of his hand King Richard rode away, leaving them all standing bareheaded in the forest glen. Then with a sigh Little John turned to his leader.

"Where now, Robin?" he asked, "since our good days are done."

"Nay," said Robin "for such as will may keep with me in our secret glade, and who keeps count of the game in Sherwood so well as the warden of the forest? So many head are my right each year, and we will have them, while since we are all rich men with the loot from Damon's ship and other small things we have won, anyone who will may hire him land or take to the towns. But the greenwood for me."

A score of them elected to leave the band and settle down, but the rest kept to their leader, and went with him to receive from the Sheriff of Nottingham the parchment deed of their pardon. There was many a smile among them at Robert de Rainault's sour face as he handed the deed to Robin, for he had far rather hanged his enemy.

How Guy of Gisbourne Tried Again

CHAPTER XVIII

~

here is an old ballad which tells that King Richard, when he pardoned Robin Hood and his band, took them to court with him to serve about him, but this cannot have been true. For Richard, landing in England after his ransom from the Austrian castle, spent but a few days in London before he went off to Lincolnshire and the Midlands to punish the worst of those who had followed John in his absence, and, when he returned to his capitol, it was but to raise money and assemble his men for the journey to France from which he never returned. He spent only three months in England, at this time. So it is much more likely that he made Robin warden of Sherwood, knowing that he who had hunted the King's deer would know how to guard them from other hunters.

He had not left England before Robert de Rainault, sore and angry over Robin's pardon, sought audience with Prince John and put before him what he called "this monstrous injustice" of the royal pardon for the outlaws. John nodded, understanding.

"Wait, Sheriff," he bade, "for my royal brother hath many matters on his hands at this time. You shall give me the names of these men, and I will send you

140

a full deed of outlawry against them, which you shall hold till I give you word to publish it." For John had not forgotten the archery contest at the Nottingham tournament, nor how Robin Hood had threatened him with one of his arrows.

So Sheriff Robert went back, while Robin, with Little John, Friar Tuck and most of the men of his band still remaining with him, took up his duties in the forest. Then, after Robert de Rainault and his brother the Abbot had had a talk, off went Abbot Hugo to Prince John, to tell the tale of his loss of fifteen hundred marks—but he did not tell how King Richard had bidden him wait for trial for his own crimes. He went back to Nottingham with a letter for his brother, bearing John's signature, and bidding him proclaim Robin Hood and his men outlaws once more.

The news came like a thunderclap to the men of the band. Much, the miller's son, whom Robin had put in charge of Locksley Farm when he claimed it back as his right, was in Nottingham when the crier proclaimed the news, and all the city buzzed with excitement over it. Much went hastening back to Locksley, for he knew that Robin himself, with Marian, were due to visit him the next day,

while there were the men about the farm to warn as well, lest they should be taken and hanged as outlaws.

It was then late spring, and Much came back toward Locksley in the dusk of the evening, but with light enough to see the gleam of armour about the homestead. Guy of Gisbourne, sent by the Abbot of St. Mary's, had laid an ambush about the place, but Much's forest training had made his eyes keen, and instead of making for Locksley he slid away into the forest, and made all the haste he could to the secret retreat in which Robin and Marian still lived with their faithful followers round them.

"Good Robin," said Much, "we are all dead men."

"Say no more," said Robin, "for there is an old proverb that dead men tell no tales, yet here you come with a tale."

"Robin, the Sheriff of Nottingham hath proclaimed us all outlawed again, for I heard it cried in the city this day."

"He did that once before, but we were not dead for it then," Robin answered composedly.

"And St. Mary's hath set an ambush round Locksley homestead," Much went on with his tale, "to catch any of us who come there."

"Right good news," Robin answered. "I will twist Master Guy his tail for him, and, if these good men are willing, we will set an ambush round his home. For if a good game is started, at least two should play at it, by all accounts."

"Robin, you seem no bit alarmed by this news," Little John remarked.

"Alarmed?" Robin said, and laughed. "Nay, for while I have been warden of the forest, I have had but a certain number of the deer allotted to me for our eating. Now we have the lot, Little John, and other things as well that we have missed since we left off being outlaws."

"What will you do, then?" Little John asked.

"Well," said Robin, "first of all we will get Friar Tuck to roast the haunches of venison that we had hung up for to-morrow, for now we may take all we like. Next, we will roll out a fresh barrel of ale, for there is a wagon train of liquor due up from Newark next week, and it shall pay full toll to us. So we shall make ourselves a right merry feast, before we go to twist the tail of Guy of Gisbourne."

Marian, seeing them talking, came out to them, and Robin put his arm round her affectionately.

"Dear girl," he said, "we are once more outlawed. Now will you that I send you to your father at Lea Castle, for safety?"

She laughed at him. "When you are tired of me, Robin, then you may send me away. Not before."

He kissed her tenderly.

"Now tell Friar Tuck to cook his hardest, for we will all feast late this night," he bade. "Bid him take venison and spare not, for all is ours again. And at dawn we will set out for Gisbourne grange, while Guy keeps watch over Locksley."

"My part, methinks, lies in the tapping of that new barrel," Little John said. "Much, come and lend me a hand with it."

"Roll out two barrels, Much," Robin Hood added, "for if Little John and the friar get at one, there will be little left in it for us."

It was, as Robin had said, late when they began their feast, but there was an air of merriment and jollity about it which had been lacking of late. Little John sang a spirited song while Robin made sweet accompaniment upon a harp. For, with King Richard overseas again, prelates and barons had felt

themselves free to do as they liked with the common people, and as the King's man Robin had had to keep within the law, and let pass many an act of tyranny that he would have checked had he been outlawed and king of Sherwood, as he was now once again.

They had barely settled to their feast when in came Will Scarlett, who, since they had had the royal pardon, had gone into partnership with old Much the miller, but now, learning that he was not safe outside Sherwood, returned to Robin's band. Friar Tuck gave him a roaring welcome.

"Hail, good Will! Come and drink with me, and eat between whiles! Here is a deer better than any we ever shot in the old days, and I know a fat herd where your bow may be useful. Come to me, good Will, and let me but pat you on the back once."

"Nay," said Scarlett, "for if you pat me, as you call it, I should have no breath left to feed with. I will sit here by Much, who eats only enough for one man, for he who shares a dish with you, Friar, must bite hard and fast if he would get a bite at all."

"So at Ravenscar," said Little John. "We had but the one venison pasty between us, and the Friar took one bite—"

"And Little John took one bite, and where was the pasty?" the Friar roared. "But there is a second cask of good ale, Will, for Little John got at the bung of the first and it is naught but an empty cask."

"Mayhap you smelt it," Scarlett suggested.

"I have a strong nose," said Friar Tuck, "but it is not strong enough to draw a bung from a cask, Will. Eat, man, for the deer are all ours."

So they feasted, right merrily, with Marian to grace their feast, and Robin Hood revolving plans for the future in his brain.

In mid-morning of the next day Guy of Gisbourne and his men tramped back, hungry and weary, from keeping useless watch on Locksley Farm, for neither Much, whom they expected to find there, nor anyone else, had appeared for them to catch. Guy looked forward to rest and refreshment at his grange before going on to report to Abbot Hugo how the outlaws had got wind of his ambush too soon, but from behind a hedge nearly a quarter of a mile distant from his place some four score heads bobbed up as he came on with his men, and a flight of arrows sang about their ears and rattled on their harness. Except for three of them who went down, two with arrows through their legs and one shot in the shoulder, Guy's men turned and bolted for cover like shot rabbits, and Guy himself followed them, cursing as he ran.

"Stout fighter," Robin remarked sarcastically. "In case he lose himself, we will light him a fire that he may see his way home when he looks round again."

And, taking half a dozen of his men while the rest kept watch for Guy and his followers, Robin marched to the grange, where the few serfs left fled at his approach, and set fire to the place. He left the ricks and cattle sheds untouched, but soon the stone house was wrapped in flames, which licked off the thatch and poured skyward in a dense column of black smoke, visible for miles round.

"Now," said Robin as he led his men away, "let Guy warm himself."

And thus ended Guy's second attempt at catching Robin Hood, which, since the grange was the property of St. Mary's Abbey, left Abbot Hugo a very angry man, swearing vengeance on Robin and his band.

The Named Arrow

CHAPTER XIX

~

ow, although Robin Hood and his men were again proclaimed outlaws, they had so many friends that it was not considered safe to
touch them in any way, for all knew that King Richard had given
them a free pardon, and only the ill-will of the Sheriff Robert and
Abbot Hugo were to blame for this second proclamation. Some day, people
said, King Richard would come back, and then Robin Hood would come to his
own again.

So the band lived a right merry life in the forest depths, for they had
won wealth enough to keep them in comfort, and added to it by an occasional
raid on people whom Robin thought not fully entitled to all they had. Thus my
Lord Bishop of Hereford came down that way after a visit to the see of York,
and Robin relieved him and his party of much good spoil, after which he tied
the Bishop to a tree and kept him there till he consented to say mass for the
outlaw band. And there was Sir Hugh of High Fell, a thieving Cumberland
baron who took the Sherwood track on his way north, and lost very heavily by it
in money and goods and armour. These were but two out of many, for Robin
never let his men remain idle.

So the time went by, until the grievous news came from overseas that King Richard had been struck down by an arrow before the castle of Chaluz, and had died of the wound, at which Robin and his men mourned for the loss of a good king and the coming of John, a bad one, to the throne. Still, with such friends as Sir Richard at Lea and his kind about them, they cared little for what the Sheriff of Nottingham or his brother the Abbot might do, and Robin was still counted king in Sherwood.

One summer morn, when King Richard had been dead over two years, one of Robin's men came to him hastily where he hunted in the forest not far from Nottingham itself. And, at the news his man brought, Robin sounded a call on his horn, and in a matter of minutes had two score of his followers round him, all armed with their bows and swords.

"Here is no time to lose," he told them, "for Robert de Rainault hath captured our Little John and takes him into Nottingham to hang him."

"Where is the Sheriff?" Will Scarlett asked.

"Now on his way to Nottingham with his prisoner," Robin answered. "There are enough of us to rescue our man, for if once he get into Nottingham jail, it will be a hard task to save him from the hangman. Let us away to the track, and meet this Sheriff once more."

As he went, he took the arrows out from his quiver and looked them over, selecting one that he had kept for years now. On it the Sheriff had written his name, when Robin had captured him and made him sign promising that if ever he moved against Robin again, so surely would that arrow be sent through his evil heart.

"I think it is time that arrow was set on the string," Robin said to himself, and put it back in the quiver carefully, apart from the rest.

Little John, it seemed, had been alone when they took him, and the man who came to Robin Hood with the news of his capture had seen the Sheriff, with a party of armed men, riding down toward Nottingham with his prisoner tied to his own saddle, with hands bound behind him. Wounded men in the party, bandaged and drooping, showed that Little John had given a good account of himself before they caught him, but he limped as the Sheriff's horse dragged him along, as if he had been wounded in the struggle.

"Sheriff Robert will not limp when I have done with him," Robin promised grimly.

They came to the track, and saw by the hoof-marks on it that the Sheriff and his men had not yet gone back to Nottingham. Then Robin placed his men, and waited a full half hour, for he was determined to save his brave man from the Sheriff's grasp.

Noon had passed before the clinking of harness and a murmur of voices warned Robin's men that the Sheriff was on his way toward them, and then they saw him, with Little John bound and dragged along by a rope that bound him to the Sheriff's horse, and nearly fifty men-at-arms following their master. Robin saw that Little John could scarcely walk, and without challenge or any word he crashed an arrow into the horse's head, so that it fell dead on the track, and the Sheriff barely got clear of it as it dropped, but drew his sword.

"Ha! Ambush!" he cried. "At them, my men—five marks a head for every one we capture."

His men were Normans, sturdy and dogged, and Robin knew that they outnumbered his own party. But Robin's second arrow dropped one of them, and six others went down under the outlaws' shooting before they drew their swords and charged in, fiercely determined on rescuing their giant comrade. It was a fight fierce and fell, like that they had fought against Damon the pirate, with no quarter on either side, and Robin said afterward that no men ever gave him and his band such fighting as these of the Sheriff over Little John, who, too weak from his wound to free himself, sat on the carcass of the horse and watched the fray.

"At them, men!" the Sheriff shouted, seeing that the outlaws held their own. "Five marks a head—fifty for Robin Hood himself."

But his men won no prisoners, for every man of Robin's party fought like a hero. Now a dozen of the Sheriff's men were down, and ten of Robin's band, and Will Scarlett, striking at one, was himself struck from behind by the Sheriff, who laid him low over the body of his own man. At that Robin found time to draw back from the fighting and get out the arrow he had kept, for this foul stroke at his man enraged him, and he had loved Will Scarlett almost as much as Little John himself.

"Remember the signed arrow, Sheriff!" he cried as he loosed the string.

The arrow sped to its mark, and crashed full in Robert de Rainault's forehead. By that time half of Robin's men were down, and more than half of the Sheriff's party, though they were more heavily armed and ready for the fight, since the outlaws had come to it in hunting trim, with no thought of a battle.

But, at the Sheriff's fall, panic seized on his men, who fled as best they could—such of them as were able to flee. Arrows followed them in their flight, and on that day Robin himself, raging at the loss of Will Scarlett, who moved no more after the Sheriff's foul stroke, accomplished one of his most noted feats of archery. For there was one of the Sheriff's men who had won almost to the gate of Nottingham itself when, from nearly a mile away, a long shaft from Robin's bow laid him lifeless, last to fall of the party who had dared to measure swords against Robin Hood and his men in fair fight.

They loosed Little John's bonds, and found him so sorely hurt that they had to carry him to their stronghold, where he was weeks recovering from his wound. Will Scarlett they buried in the greenwood, and Robin mourned over the loss of a gallant fighter and true friend. Eighteen of Robin's men, it is said, died that day, while of the Sheriff's party near on thirty never came back to tell the tale.

But those who did win back to Nottingham told that they had nearly exterminated the outlaws, and that Robin himself had been sorely wounded. For they had to cover up their defeat by giving the number of their assailants as far greater than it was, and so the word went round that the outlaws of Sherwood were broken men, their leader sorely wounded, and their numbers so reduced that the forest might easily be cleared of them.

Among those who heard this story was Abbot Hugo, brother of the dead Sheriff, who, when he had said masses for the repose of Robert de Rainault's soul, after attending his funeral at Nottingham, called to him Guy of Gisbourne for a conference.

"Time after time I have sent you against this outlaw, Guy," he said, "and each time he hath shamed you. But now, I think, we have him."

"You would have me go after him again, Lord Abbot?" Guy asked.
The Abbot nodded. "We will have vengeance for my brother's death," he said, "the more so since the arrow that slew him, being marked with his name, points clearly to murder by this Robin Hood."

"How will you that I take him." Guy asked. "For if I go hunting in Sherwood for him, I may hunt a year, and never find a sign of him. He knows the forest too well."

"Nay," said Hugo, "that is work wasted. But do you get together our men-at-arms, of whom we can muster over forty, and say nothing of our intent. I will cause it to be given out that, at the end of next week, I am sending the tax money for our King John down to Nottingham, for that money must be sent. It shall go under guard of five armed men only, with half a dozen of our friars."

"Ah!" said Guy. "That will be the bait."

The Abbot nodded. "That will be the bait," he agreed, "and you shall be the trap. For we know by all reports that there are not a score of these outlaws left now, and you shall follow on the party with the gold by half an hour. When Robin Hood and his men are busy over the spoil, you and your men can fall on them, and strike and spare not, for my brother's murder calls for vengeance."

Guy nodded agreement. "I have some vengeance to take, too," he said. "Do you give me notice when the convoy is to start, Lord Abbot, and I will be there with the men."

Guy of Gisbourne's Last Attempt

CHAPTER XX

~

he sun shone brightly on Sherwood's glades when Abbot Hugo sent his convoy, as he had planned, toward Nottingham, confident that Robin Hood and his men would come out after it, and thus render themselves easy prey for Guy of Gisbourne and the party who followed on after the pack mules. And, up to a point, the plan worked well enough, for when the friars with the mules were still two miles away from Nottingham gate, a body of outlaws broke out of the forest shades and surrounded them.

"Now stand, you shavelings," said Friar Tuck, who led the attacking party, "for that cargo looks to me as if it needs overhauling."

"Shaveling yourself," retorted Anselm, Abbot Hugo's clerk, who was in charge of the party. "Here be holy relics that we bear to St. Ninian's church in Nottingham, against the festival of harvest. Dare not to commit sacrilege by laying hands on them!"

"Relics?" the jolly Friar queried. "What relics?"

"Here we bear in a casket the fingernail of St. Bridget, and some clippings from the hair of the holy Saint Augustine himself, to say nothing of a shoe lace said to have been given by King Hengist himself to Saint Wilfrid. Dare not to lay hands on such sacred cargo."

"Much," said Friar Tuck, "while I keep an arrow on the string in case this sanctimonious clerk should have arms under his cassock, do you overhaul his fingernails and shoe laces and hair clippings, and see what else there may be in the packs. For neither hair nor nail nor shoe lace are enough to burden six mules, unless the holy Augustine grew haystacks on his head."

"Vile sacrilege!" said Anselm, listening all the while for Guy of Gisbourne and his men, who should have been close behind. "Such impiety, recreant friar, will bring its own punishment."

"Recreant?" roared the good Friar, angrily. "Much, take me that long nose of his between your fingers, and twist it till he take back the word, for if I were not a better son of Holy Church than any one of Hugo's shavelings I would never draw bow at another deer. Tweak the nose, good Much."

Much needed no second invitation. He took a strong grip on Anselm's nose and tweaked it till the tears streamed down the clerk's cheeks and he howled for mercy loudly.

"Now am I recreant?" Friar Tuck asked sternly.

"Nay, Friar, you are as good a churchman as my nose—as any of us!" Anselm answered fearfully.

"Saints, what a grip this knave hath!"

"Do you call me a knave?" Much asked fiercely, and reached for the nose again. Anselm leaped back.

"Nay, good fellow, 'twas a slip of the tongue. I mean no ill."

"Stand there, then, while we overhaul the mules' loads," Much bade. "We will leave you your shoe laces and fingernails, and all gear of that sort, so fear not for them."

They laid out the stores that the mules carried, and found good flour ground in Abbot Hugo's mills, a couple of bags of gold marks, store of cloth and fine linen, and sundry other rich goods that Abbot Hugo had sent, never doubting that Guy and his men would see them safely through, as presents for the new Sheriff of Nottingham, Simon Ganmere, who had been appointed in consequence of Robert de Rainault's death at the hands of Robin Hood. There was also a letter that Anselm the clerk carried, which Much, having searched the clerk, handed to Friar Tuck to read.

The friar read it aloud for the outlaws to hear.

To Simon Ganmere, greeting and good will, from our Abbey of
St. Mary's. I send with this sundry presents, and bespeak your

presence at my Abbey to a banquet that I will hold on any day that may please you. If things fall out as I have planned them, this day will the villain outlaw, Robin Hood, be captured or killed by my steward, Guy of Gisbourne, and if he should be captured alive it is my will that Guy bring him to you at Nottingham, that you may hang him over the city gate, as warning to all rogues of his kind. Also I think that Guy my man will dispose of most of the outlaws who yet remain.

But, since some may escape to be a terror to honest men, I trust that you, Sheriff, will root them out of the forest and burn their hold, so that the ways may be free again when we have cause to travel by Sherwood on our errands. And most heartily do I trust that Guy of Gisbourne may take this Robin Hood alive, for it would please me most mightily if he were hanged like a common felon, rather than killed in fight.

Now again I send you right hearty greeting, and the hope that you may accept these poor presents of mine with my good will toward you. Given at our Abbey of St. Mary's by Hugo, Abbot.

"A right cheerful epistle," said Friar Tuck, when he had finished reading, "and I doubt not that it will please our Robin to hear it read again. Put all the goods back on the mules, lads, and trouble not whether there is a stray fingernail or a shoe lace or two over, after this. And we, being bursting with good will, like Abbot Hugo, will truss these shaven rascals like chickens, with gags to stop their squealing, and place them gently away from the track, lest they should be found too easily, while we go and see what our good Robin and the rest of the band are doing."

Six men went off with the mules to the outlaws' secret hold, while Anselm and the other monks, submitting to being bound and gagged because they could not help it, still hoped to see Guy of Gisbourne ride down on the outlaws and put them to flight, before all was done. But they waited in vain, for there was no sound nor sign of Guy or any man.

A mile behind them, Guy of Gisbourne had led on twenty mounted men, and thirty men on foot, till they came to a point where not more than three of them could ride abreast, and the undergrowth on either side was too dense for a man to force his way through. Suddenly, as they rode, a great tree trunk crashed down across the track before them, barring the way, since it was too big for a horse to leap, and as the horses shied back in alarm a second trunk fell with a thud behind, so that they were in a sort of pen, horse and foot together. Ahead of them, beyond the foremost fallen trunk, Robin Hood stepped out into view, and a dozen crossbows were instantly levelled at him. But not a bolt was shot, for a flight of great arrows whizzed before the crossbowmen could take aim, and Abbot Hugo was short of a dozen men that moment.

"And so for the next man who would shoot," said Robin calmly, as he advanced close to the great log across the way. "'Tis a great while since we two have had a word with each other, Guy, and I have a mind to talk with you alone, with a sword or two between us to point our speech."

Now Guy, who had counted on outnumbering Robin's men by two to one, saw outlaws swarm out from the forest depths to watch over their leader, and knew himself and his men outnumbered, while already he had seen how deadly were the arrows of his opponents.

"I yield me," he said sullenly. "You have outwitted me again, and I would not waste the lives of good men any more."

"Have no fear," Robin assured him, "for my men can take care of themselves. No good men will suffer, though those Norman hogs behind you may be sorry for themselves, if you choose to fight."

"Robin!" called Friar Tuck from behind him, waddling up with the letter he had taken from Anselm in his hand. "Hold them yet a minute while I read you this. 'Tis from Abbot Hugo to the new Sheriff at Nottingham."

He read the letter aloud, translating it to Norman-French as he read, so that Guy of Gisbourne's men might hear and understand it. Robin and most of his men understood that tongue as well as English, and Robin's face darkened as he heard what Hugo had written.

"There is a new face on this business," he said, "for this talk of a hanging is not to my taste. Guy of Gisbourne, you have heard?"

"Aye, I have heard," Guy answered, "and stand by it."

"For my part, I have a mind to end this matter here," Robin said with deadly calm, for the letter had angered him past bearing. "Now do you get down and climb over that log with your sword, leaving your men where they are, for I have no quarrel with them, poor fools. Here you and I will fight it out, with these men of mine to see fair play, and so shall we end this long quarrel once and for all."

"And if I win the fight, what happens to me then?" Guy asked.

"You go back to Abbot Hugo, and tell him how you have made an end of me," Robin Hood answered.

"And if I will not fight you so?" Guy asked again.

"Then in the hearing of your men I name you coward, unworthy to be followed by the meanest knave that breathes," Robin said fiercely. "Twice you have come against me, and twice have I let you go back alive to your

master. Now, this third time, we settle it for all time, Guy. Get down from your horse and come out, sword to sword."

After one more moment's hesitation Guy dismounted, handed his horse over to his men, and clambered over the log, after which he drew his sword. Robin, with his men in a ring about him, faced his old enemy.

"To the death, Guy," he said.

"To the death," Guy of Gisbourne echoed.

Then they set to, fighting warily at first, so that the great blades sliddered along each other with a grinding noise as they guarded each other's blows and thrusts. And it chanced that Robin trod on a thick twig as he stepped back, so that it rolled under his foot, and he slipped a little. The point of Guy's sword just nicked his neck above his doublet, drawing blood.

"Aha!" said Guy. "Nearly!"

"Nearly, fool, is not quite," Robin responded. "Guard there!"

And Guy was in time, but only just in time, to save himself from Robin's recovery and resulting thrust.

Now they had fought a good ten minutes, and both were breathing hard, for the work grew hot and fierce. Presently Robin leaped in the air as Guy tried the old Norse trick of sweeping at his knees, and by that the steward of St. Mary's sealed his own doom. For, ere he could get his blade aloft, Robin struck home, and with one great backhanded blow laid Guy of Gisbourne dead.

He stood back. "An end," he said. "Peace to him, though he served a bad master, and himself had no pity on those he ruled."

"And next, mighty Robin Hood?" Friar Tuck asked.

"Haul up the logs to let these men and horses go," Robin answered, "but first strip them to their shirts, as once before we did with the men whom Guy of Gisbourne led against us. Then let them take him and these other dead back to St. Mary's Abbey, and pin that letter of the Abbot's on the breast of dead Guy, that he may know how his message hath fared at our hands."

The Last Arrow

CHAPTER XXI

~

ow came peace in Sherwood, for King John and the barons were too busy fighting each other to spare men for clearing off Robin Hood's band, and Simon Ganmere, the new Sheriff of Nottingham, though he sent bodies of men after them once or twice, got worsted so much that, rather than make himself a laughingstock, he left them alone. Yet out of his attempts, and Robin's method of tricking him and his men, came so many merry adventures that ballads were made of them later, and the outlaws came to hold Simon in such small regard that they went into Nottingham and dealt in the markets there almost openly.

So the years passed, and the merry men hunted the deer and took toll of prelates and barons as they would, holding feasts to which they dragged unwilling abbots and even bishops, who paid for their entertainment as Robin willed, since he knew that the money he took was squeezed out of some unfortunate serf or freeman, and that the people from whom he took it had not even as much right to it as himself, since he was always willing to help man or woman in need. Great days and great adventures they had, of which the memory has come down in old songs which the minstrels used to sing all over England.

But in St. Mary's Abbey, Hugo de Rainault remembered the death of his brother at Robin Hood's hands; he remembered, too, how Robin had set free Sir Richard at Lea, and so had shamed him before King Richard; he remembered that, if Robin had not lent Sir Richard the money to redeem his bond, Sir Richard's manor would have been added to his own lands, and that by marrying Maid Marian Robin had prevented her lands from coming to his friend Sir

Isambart. Altogether, Abbot Hugo had a long count against the great outlaw, and he nursed his hate and waited, meanwhile growing old.

He could see no way of getting even with his enemy, for never could any man find the way to Robin's secret glade in the depths of Sherwood; those who knew it would not betray the men who were their friends, and, lacking that knowledge, Hugo knew it was useless to send men into the forest depths. While he brooded and grew old the world went its accustomed way; Magna Carta was signed by the unwilling King, giving to all men such liberties as they had not had before; King John died of vexation after his disastrous march across the Lincolnshire Wash, and the boy King Henry came to the throne with his barons warring round him. Still the outlaw band throve in Sherwood, and hunted the deer in its glades.

Abbot Hugo was quite an old man when he was told, one day, that a chapman or pedlar desired to see him, and bade that the man should be admitted to his presence. In came a thin little man with his pack on his back, and, when he had put down the pack and looked at Hugo with narrow, crafty eyes, the Abbot stared hard at him.

"That," he said, "should be the face of Roger le Gran, if the years had not changed it so."

"It is, Abbot," Roger, called "the Cruel," answered. "Once a knight, but, since Robin Hood and his men burnt out Castle Belame, a beggared man living how I can."

"Well," the Abbot said, "I cannot help you, Roger, for that same Robin hath stripped me of so much of my wealth that I am but a poor man now."

"But how if I could help you?" Roger asked. "You cannot hate this Robin more than I hate him. What if I find you a way to his hold, and guide your men there to destroy it?"

"Can you do this?" Hugo asked eagerly.

Roger nodded. "I think I see a way," he answered. "What will you give me if I do it?"

"If I knew that all the band of them were destroyed," Hugo answered slowly, "I would give half the spoil that they have amassed, and five hundred gold marks as well—enough to make you the richest man between here and Nottingham, friend Roger."

Roger nodded. "I do not know the way to their hold yet," he said, "but I think there is a way by which I may find it. It needs but that I travel there and return once, for I never forget a road I have trodden."

"But how will you get there?" Hugo asked.

"Harkye, Abbot," Roger responded, "and I will tell my plan."

So they talked a long while, and Abbot Hugo sent for food and wine, and fed his man so well that the monks wondered how it came about that a mere chapman should be so much honoured by their proud Abbot.

Next day the outlaws had fed full well in their glade, as was their custom, and Friar Tuck, fatter and more jovial than ever, had declared that if he had only drunk two quarts less of ale with his venison, Little John would never have beaten him at the good game of quarter-staff. Down into the glade, toward evening, came Will the Pedlar, an old friend of the band, who often brought his pack to see if they would buy of him, and generally brought them news as well. With him came a stranger, also with a pack on his back, at sight of whom Little John stepped forward.

"How now, Will?" Little John asked. "You know well that no strangers may learn the way to our retreat."

"But this is an honest rascal, your worship," Will answered, "and he hath a goodly store of right curious trinkets, Arabian daggers, a hunting knife that the Soldan of Syria used, and like marvels. I vouch for him being a right good man, and safe to bring to your hold."

"Let be, then, since he is here," Little John growled, "but you are surety for his honesty, remember."

One thing that Will the Pedlar did not tell Little John was that the stranger had given him five good gold marks for permission to accompany him to the glade. The newcomer spread out his wares, and soon had the outlaws bargaining with him, while the wives of such as lived married in the glade came to buy ornaments, which the chapman offered at such ridiculously cheap rates that presently the news came to Marian, Robin's wife.

"I think I will go and see this chapman," she said, "in case he have any trinkets left that I should like."

The evening was growing old, then, and, as she went out from the home that she had shared with Robin for years now, she saw the strange chapman rolling up his pack, as if to depart. But she went up to him, in case any of his goods should be left unsold.

"Good chapman," she asked courteously, "may I not see your wares?"

He looked up at her, and instantly she knew the face of Roger the Cruel, which she had last seen when Isambart held her prisoner in Evil Hold. No other among the outlaw band knew his face, for always they had seen him in armour, and with visor down, but Marian knew him, and at sight of his evil eyes she turned to cry out a warning. But Roger leaped at her, drawing his dagger, and struck her down, so that her cry was a scream of pain.

At the sound men came to the doors of their huts in the glade, and Robin, knowing that it was Marian who had cried, snatched at his bow and ran out to aid her. He saw her lying helpless, and saw the figure of a man running madly toward the cliff path in the dusk, and at that he put an arrow on the string. The distance was great and the light uncertain, but the arrow was sped by the best archer who ever drew string beside his ear in all England.

The speeding arrow took Roger in the shoulder as he brushed by a sapling, and pinned him to the tree in such fashion that he could not move for the pain that movement gave him. By this time a dozen men were running toward Marian, but Robin, easily outdistancing them, pointed to the figure on the cliff path.

"Let be," he said, "and fetch that man back. I will see to my own wife while you get him."

And he ran to Marian, lifting her in his arms. Her wound, he could tell, was too deep for any aid to save her, and she herself knew that she was dying. She smiled up at him.

"This, methinks, is our farewell, lover of mine," she said weakly, "for in a little time I shall be gone. But before I go, I would thank you for all the happy years."

Robin bent his head and kissed her. "Dear wife," he said brokenly, "I had looked for many more happy years together, but now is life robbed of its chief joy, and I go sorrowing all my days."

"There is left you green Sherwood, Robin mine," she told him, "and I shall watch over you. Now call our Friar that I may have the last rites of the Church, and do you hold me."

So Robin held her while Friar Tuck, with tears running down his cheeks, administered to her, and then left them. What they said to each other in the last minutes no man knew, except for one sentence of hers that Robin told Little John and Friar Tuck after.

"So, she said, she would have had it," he said, "to die in the heart of the greenwood with my arms round her, and the evening light fading. And never had man truer or more loyal wife than this my Marian, whom I shall mourn until I, too, die and go to join her."

Now, before the light had altogether gone, they brought back Roger the Cruel, but by that time Robin had borne the body of Marian away, and returned to stand with folded arms, grimly waiting to face the murderer. While he waited, Will the Pedlar flung himself at the outlaw's feet.

"Mercy, Robin!" he whined, "for I thought him a true man, else I had not let him come with me."

"This mercy," Robin answered calmly. "Get you gone, nor ever let me see your face again, or I may remember how my wife died through you."

Will slunk away, and fled out of Nottinghamshire altogether soon after, for the story went about how he had brought to the outlaws' hold the man who murdered the queen of Sherwood.

But Robin and his men took Roger the Cruel and marched through the night with him, for they had found on him a paper by which the Abbot of St. Mary's promised him half the spoil of the secret glade, and five hundred marks as well, in return for guidance to their hiding place. Roger had not trusted the Abbot's word, but had claimed the paper before he would go to search out the way.

As they went, Robin's men hewed down great poles from the forest trees, which they took with them, and, fifty yards from the gate of St. Mary's Abbey, they set up a gallows of these poles, and on it hanged Roger the Cruel, with the Abbot's parchment of promise sewn on his breast, that all men might see. Across the foot of it Friar Tuck had written at Robin's bidding:

"This doom to Abbot Hugo's hireling murderer. When next Abbot Hugo goes abroad, the doom will find him, too."

After which threat, Abbot Hugo never left the Abbey grounds, for he knew that Robin Hood kept his word always.

But, after Marian's death, things were never the same in the glade, for all had loved her, and all mourned her loss, while Robin Hood himself was inconsolable. He divided up the wealth they had won among the men of his band, and bade them reckon themselves free to go where they would.

Some went to Sir Richard at Lea, now grown old, but still giving every man of Robin's a welcome. Some went to the wars and fought in the battles that lasted till Simon de Montfort fell at Evesham, and some hired land and settled down to tell of the good days that had been in Sherwood.

When all was done, and Friar Tuck had gone to hermitage nearby a noble trout stream and within bowshot of certain deer of Sherwood, Robin took down his bow and quiver and buckled his sword about his waist, while Little John watched and wondered.

"How now, good Robin?" Little John asked.

"Wherever the winds may blow me, or chance call me, there I shall go," Robin answered. "Do you make shift as have the rest, for our good days in Sherwood are done now that we grow old."

"Where you go, I go," said Little John, "for we have been friends too long to part by any wish of mine, until death parts us."

"We will go north, then," Robin said, "and I will count I have not lived in vain if you set such store by my friendship, good John."

"Think of the times we have known together," Little John said wistfully. "The good days when we sent Guy's band home in their shirts, and tricked the Sheriff and all the rest, and burned Evil Hold—"

"And made an end of Damon the Pirate," Robin supplemented.

"And how great King Richard talked with you and gave you pardon, and how we spoiled the Abbot—aye, Robin, we have known too much together ever to part company."

So, with Much, the miller's son, they went north, toward the Yorkshire border, but the spirit was out of bold Robin Hood since his dear wife's death,

and sickness fell on him as they travelled, so that when they came to Kirklees Abbey he besought the Abbess Elizabeth to give him shelter and a bed till he should be well enough to go on his way, at which she gave him a bed in a cell and tended him, while Little John and others slept before the door, lest there should be any treachery. Twice the Abbess bled Robin for his sickness, but it seemed to do him little good, and while he lay there the Abbot Hugo of St.

Mary's got word that he was in power of the Abbess. At that Hugo wrote to the woman, who, though he did not know it, was sister to Robin's mother, else Robin had not reckoned himself safe there, since Kirklees was under the government of Abbot Hugo of St. Mary's.

A day after she had received Hugo's letter, the Abbess came to Robin's bedside and looked down at him thoughtfully.

"Nephew Robin, I must bleed you again, if you would get well."

"Be it as you will," he answered weakly.

She took a lancet and opened a vein, though in her heart she knew well that he was too weak for any more bleeding. Yet Abbot Hugo had laid a command on her, and though Robin was her own sister's son she obeyed.

Something in her eyes told him her intent, and he called out weakly, at which Little John, who had been waiting outside for the Abbess to go, entered the room. Robin lay by the window in a pool of blood, his face very white.

"A boon, a boon!" cried Little John, with tears streaming from his eyes. "Let me slay this wretch and burn her body in the ruins of this place."

His master answered him with a voice from the grave: " 'Twas always my part never to hurt a woman, John. I will not let you do so now. Look to my wishes instead. Marian's grave—it is to be kept well and honorably. For me, dear heart, bury me nearby, in some quiet grave. I could not bear another journey."

Little John sought to lift him up. "Give me my bow," said Robin, suddenly, "and a good true shaft." He took them from John's shaking hands, and then, leaning heavily against his friend's sobbing breast, Robin Hood flew his last arrow out through the window, far away into the deep green of the trees.

A swift remembrance lit up the dying man's face. "Ah, well," he cried, "Marian, my heart...and the day when first we met. And she is gone, and my last arrow is flown. It is the end." He fell back into Little John's arms. "Bury me," he murmured, faintly, "where my arrow hath fallen. There lay a green sod under my head and another beneath my feet, and let my bow be at my side."

His voice became presently silent, as though something had snapped within him. His head dropped gently upon Little John's shoulder.

"You sleep," whispered Little John, again and again, trying to make himself believe it was so. "You are asleep, Robin—let me lay you quietly upon your bed."

So died Robin of Locksley under treacherous hands. Near by Kirklees Abbey they laid to his last rest this bravest of all brave men—the most fearless champion of freedom that the land had ever known.

Robin Hood is dead, and no man can say truly where his grave may be. At the least it but holds his bones. His name lives in our ballads, our history, our hearts—so long as the English tongue is known.

~ Acknowledgments ~

We wish to thank the following properties whose cooperation has made this unique collection possible. All care has been taken to trace ownership of these selections and to make a full acknowledgment. If any errors or omissions have occurred, they will be corrected in subsequent editions, provided notification is sent to the compiler. And with deepest appreciation we wish to thank The Robin Hood Society of West London for supplying information on the works by unknown illustrators.

Honor C. Appleton [George G. Harrap & Company Ltd.: London, 1931]. Page 79.

Robert Ball [Charles Scribner's Sons: New York, 1933]. Pages 13, 53.

Thomas Bewick [From *Ritson's Robin Hood,* England, 1795]. Pages 23, 59, 67, 80.

Frances Brundage [The Saalfield Publishing Co.: Akron, Ohio, n.d.]. Pages 9, 62, 77, 114, 130, 139, 157, 164.

Walter Crane [Edinburgh Publishing Company: London, 1912]. Pages 29, 33, 52, 84, 90, 98, 120, 127, 136, 138, 152, 158, 168.

C. A. Davis [McLoughlin Brothers: New York, circa 1885]. Spine and pages 4, 55, 64, 88, 94, 100, 106, 147.

Gaston de Foix [Bibliotheque Nationale: Paris, Early 15th century]. Page 21.

H. J. Ford [Longmans, Green and Company: London, 1902]. Pages 135, 171.

Charlotte Harding [Publisher Unknown: London, 1903]. Page 160.

Francesco Hayez [*Maid Marian's Kiss,* 1859]. Page 143.

I. K. [Young Folks Library, Hall & Locke Company: Boston, 1902]. Table of contents and page 11.

Nathaniel Johnson [*The Grave-slab at Kirklees,* 1665]. Page 169.

S. Lagneau [Librairie Plon: Paris, n.d.]. Page 113.

G. Laivson [The Saalfield Publishing Co.: Akron, Ohio, n.d.]. Page 86.

Patrick Nicolle [The Thames Publishing Co.: London, n.d.]. Page 146.

Lucy Fitch Perkins [Frederick A. Stokes Company: New York, 1906]. Front flap and pages 6, 8, 66, 74, 89, 118, 133, 148, 167.

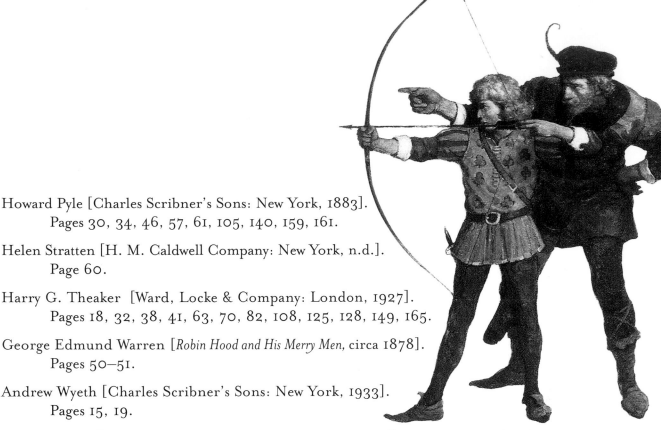

Howard Pyle [Charles Scribner's Sons: New York, 1883].
    Pages 30, 34, 46, 57, 61, 105, 140, 159, 161.

Helen Stratten [H. M. Caldwell Company: New York, n.d.].
    Page 60.

Harry G. Theaker [Ward, Locke & Company: London, 1927].
    Pages 18, 32, 38, 41, 63, 70, 82, 108, 125, 128, 149, 165.

George Edmund Warren [*Robin Hood and His Merry Men*, circa 1878].
    Pages 50–51.

Andrew Wyeth [Charles Scribner's Sons: New York, 1933].
    Pages 15, 19.

N. C. Wyeth [David McKay Publisher: Philadelphia, 1917]. Pages 10, 37, 69, 87, 95,
    104, 144, 170, 173.

N. C. Wyeth [Charles Scribner's Sons: New York, 1933]. Page 93.

Gwen White [Publisher unknown, n.d.]. Page 43.

Unknown illustrator [Pierce Egan: London, 1840]. Page 7.

Unknown illustrator [Robin Hood card game, London, circa 1860]. Endpapers and page 12.

Unknown illustrator [From *A True Tale of Robin Hood,* W. Thackeray: England, 1687]. Page 17.

Unknown illustrator [From "The Gest of Robyn Hode," *Wynkyn de Worde*, England,
    circa 1492–1534]. Page 25.

Unknown illustrator [From *Luttrell Psalter,* England, circa 1340]. Page 39.

Unknown illustrator [Engravings of twelfth-century knights, London,
    circa 1840–1860]. Pages 45, 47, 117, 119.

Unknown illustrator [*Long Bowman,* England, 15th century]. Page 73.

Unknown illustrator [From "Roxburghe Ballads," England, 1600]. Page 97.

Unknown illustrator [Bayeux Tapestry, circa 1250]. Page 122.

Unknown illustrator [Chapbook, England, circa 1766]. Page 129.

Unknown illustrator [Redwing shoe ad, circa 1930]. Back cover and page 141.

Unknown illustrator [Comic book cover, circa 1940]. Front cover and page 151.

Unknown illustrator [Myllar prints, England, 1508]. Page 154.

GEORGE.A.GREEN

MAID MARIAN

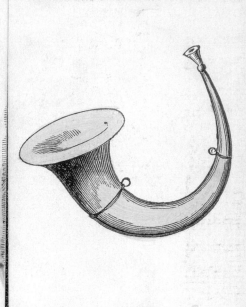

MUCH the MILLER'S SON

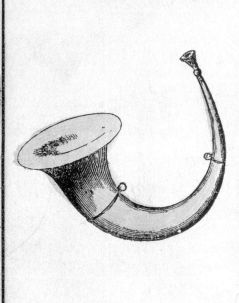

FRIAR TUCK

FLEET FOOT

ALLEN·A·DALE

FIRM FOOT